Luck

4CLOVER SERIES BOOK ONE

Shauna X

SHAUNA MC DONNELL

Shaunamcdonnell.com

Copyright

ISBN: 9781694222343

Dedications

This book is for the people who didn't believe in me.
Luckily for me... I believed in myself.
[Insert middle finger emoji here]

To Andrew, I know you may never read this, (even though you promised you would — when you had the time) but none the less, the support you've shown me throughout this process was nothing short of magical. I couldn't have asked for a better man to walk this life beside. The love you give me, and our boys, amazes me every day. Thank you for being you.

To Holly, you claimed Cian as your book boyfriend from the very first pages, this is me gifting him to you.

Author's Note

This book is written in British English, spellings may differ from American English.

A lot of my characters have Irish names. So, I've made a pronunciation chart.

Cian (Ke-ane)

Cillian (Kil-e-an)

Ciaran (Kier-on)

Conor (Conn-or)

Croí (K-ree)

Sean (Sh-aun)

My goal was to make this book as interactive as possible; each chapter has a song for a sub-title. If there is anything, I love more than reading, it's music. The playlist is available on Spotify: Luck, Boys of 4Clover. Happy listening.

About the Author

Shauna lives in the small, town land of Oldtown, North County Dublin; with her partner and her two little boys. She always loved to read, to escape reality between the pages of a good book. Her other hobbies include singing, art, all things spiritual, song writing and binge-watching Netflix series. She loves slogan t-shirts and mugs with sarcastic sayings. Her readers have described her works as laugh out loud romance, with a dash of tears and a slap of reality. If she is not reading or writing you will find her at home, earphones in, singing and dancing around the kitchen. She believes we all have a little light inside us, but it's up to us to let it shine. *Luck* is her first novella; it is book one of the Boys of 4Clover Series.

"Don't think there are no second chances. Life always offers you a second chance... it's called tomorrow."

Nicholas Sparks

Chapter One

Ella

"*V*ALENTINE'S DAY CAN GO SUCK A DICK!"

With a frustrated groan, I burst through the door of my apartment causing my roommate, Cassie, to leap from the couch.

"Jesus Christ, Ella! You scared the Cookie Dough right out of me." Cassie's hand flies to her chest. "What happened to your date? Where's Jake?"

I set my beloved black leather Michael Kors bag on the counter. With a weighty sigh, I saunter over to the couch, where my best friend has drowned her single status in a tub of Ben & Jerry's for most of the day, binge-watching re-runs of "Pretty Little Liars" on Netflix.

"Who needs a man when I can ogle Ezra Fitz?" she had declared previously this evening.

Cassie and I met two years ago, at the start of our freshman year here at UCLA. We roomed together that first semester and instantly became BFFs. *Best-*

Fucking-Friends.

We have been inseparable since the day we met. She is the yin to my yang. She's a tall leggy blonde, I'm a small curvy brunette, and even though we are complete opposites in the looks department, our personalities are extremely similar. She understands I don't come with a filter because neither does she.

I pat the space next to me, silently urging her to sit down beside me. She takes a seat, curling her legs underneath her, preparing for my explanation.

"Oh, I'll tell you where he was: in between some blonde's legs. He literally had his face planted right between her thighs," I declare.

"No," Cassie gasps. She does nothing to shield the expression of disgust on her perfect, heart-shaped face.

"Oh, yes, and do you know what he had the audacity to say? *Sorry, babe, I wasn't expecting you till eight,*" I taunt, giving my best Jake impression.

Cassie's eyebrows are near reaching her hairline at this stage. "You've got to be joking! What a douche-nugget!"

I stretch back against the couch and stare up at the ceiling fan. *Why can't I ever choose a nice guy?*

I side-glance over at Cassie. She's got devilment shining in her bright blue eyes. She hops up from the couch and claps her hands. "Ella May Andrews, as your best friend, I will not allow you to sit here in that hot little dress and wallow in self-pity. We, my dear, are going out."

I take in what she is wearing; she's got her

Minnie Mouse pyjama pants on with her UCLA hoodie. Her long blonde hair heaped into a messy bun on top of her head.

"Are you going out like that?" I question, struggling to keep back the snicker that's forcing its way up my throat. Cassie is gorgeous in everything, but those PJ's, have had better days.

"Certainly not. Give me twenty minutes, and I'll be good as new." She winks at me before skipping towards her bedroom.

As I sit waiting for Cassie, I think back over the past few months I've spent with Jake. How did I not see this coming? Were we not as serious as I thought? He told me he loved me, but clearly, that was just another lie in our so-called relationship. God, I'm so mad at myself right now. How did I not suspect he was messing around with other girls? All the signs were there. The late-night *study groups,* the random late-night texts from *his sister.* Does he even have a sister? Who knows? I won't believe a single word that leaves his mouth, especially after what I witnessed this evening. I am done with men for a while. That's it. I'm staying a single pringle.

|***|

Half an hour and a bottle of hairspray later, we walk into Jar's, a local student bar right off UCLA campus. Jar's Bar has been the go-to spot ever since Sinners played there a few years back. They were a few UCLA students who formed a band in their freshmen year; one night they were performing their regular set and some big shot record producer wandered in. I heard through the grapevine he signed them on the spot. They still play in Jar's now and again, so everyone comes here hoping to catch a glimpse of America's newest rock band.

Once we make our way past the horde of bouncers, we head inside. The bar is fully decked out for Valentine's Day. I take in all the tacky decorations. It looks like Cupid chewed the place up and spat it out. Everywhere I look there are lovey-dovey couples; hearts and roses cover every surface. I let out a sigh and turn to Cassie.

"Maybe this wasn't such a good idea?" I question. She opens her mouth to reply but we're interrupted by what I can only describe as a replica of Danny DeVito in an adult size diaper. Does he think he looks like Cupid? *Talk about over-kill.*

"Hello Ladies, Welcome to our first ever Love Locks singles' night. Here are your locks. All you must do is find the man who holds the key. You never know — he might be the man of your dreams."

The lock hangs on a piece of red ribbon so we can place it around our necks. Baby Cupid DeVito's face lights up, a creepy grin reaching his eyes when he sees us put the locks in place. Finally, he strolls off to find his next victims.

My eyes scan the room. Everyone looks to be having fun: people are dancing, the bar is jam-packed, the sound of laughter filling the air. My gaze lands on a couple to the right of the door. *Fuck my life!* Could tonight get any worse? Jake is here with Skanky McSkank, they are now sucking the faces off each other like they're the latest freaking Dyson model. *Great!* This is exactly how I wanted to spend my Valentine's Day. *Not.*

My heart tightens in my chest at the sight, how could he be so cruel? I gave him my virginity, something I can never get back, but clearly, he doesn't give a single shit. I fight to hide the gut-wrenching feeling from forming, the one that comes with seeing someone I cared about, stomping on my heart. *I am stronger than this.* I swallow down the ball of anxiety rising from my stomach. *Deep breaths, Ella. You can do this... Jake who?*

"Ella." The sound of Cassie's voice calling my name snaps me out of my self-pep talk. She places her hand on my shoulder, gently turning me around so I don't have to see my boyfriend — I mean my now ex-boyfriend — playing tonsil hockey with Bimbo Barbie.

"I'm sorry, El. You shouldn't have to witness that. Do you want to go home?" Cassie asks, her voice full of sympathy.

I force myself to stand a little taller. I have as much right to be here as he does. "No," I reply. "Screw them. They can have each other. I'm here now, and I am determined to enjoy myself. I am not wasting another minute of my time on Jake Saunders. Why don't you go find us a table up near the band? I'll go get us some drinks." I try my best to push down the emotions that come with seeing my boyfriend of five months lip-locked with someone who isn't me, but I can't deny the tightening in my solar plexus. *Fuck you, Jake. Fuck you very much.*

I make my way through the growing crowd, eventually reaching the bar to order a round of drinks. Luckily enough, the bartender is in my dance class and she serves me quickly. "Hey, El. What can I get you?"

"Oh hey, Emily! I didn't know you worked here. Can I get two beers and two tequilas please?"

"Rough day?" she questions.

"Oh, you have no idea." We chat a little more while she makes up my order before saying our goodbyes.

Have you ever tried to balance two beers and two shots of tequila while making your way across a crowded bar in 6-inch heels? It's no joke, let me tell you.

I'm just about to reach the small round table Cassie found to the right of the stage when my foot slips on some spilt liquid on the hardwood floor, causing my body to jerk forward.

The drinks I was artfully carrying go flying from my hands. *Thump.* I slam straight into a giant wall of rock-hard muscle. I look up at the shithead that made me spill my drinks all over my new red dress.

"Hey! Watch where you're going, ass... holy mother of all orgasms."

Did I say that out loud?

My gaze slowly travels up over the dark grey t-shirt that is clinging to his wide hard chest. I can easily make out the shape of his abs through his now wet t-shirt. My first thought is: *Thank you, tequila.* My second: *Good god, did Michelangelo carve this man?*

I try to take a step backwards when his two very strong, very tattooed arms wrap around my waist and pull me in tighter. I look up at the six-foot-something man in front of me. When my eyes land on his face, I see the most beautiful man I've ever seen. *Sweet baby Jesus.*

My gaze wanders to his full pair of lips, which I'm sure could kiss me stupid, and along with his chiselled jawline covered in the right amount of stubble, they erase every brain cell I have.

His messy hair is slightly long, jet black like coal, and it looks like he has been running his fingers through it. His eyes lock onto mine, and they're as impressive as the rest of him — if not more so. They look like a stormy night, navy blue with flecks of steel grey.

The reaction my body has to this man is one I have never felt before.

Goosebumps prickle along my skin, his presence sending my stomach into a frenzy — butterflies do not do justice to what this sexy stranger is making me feel.

Mr. Orgasm's chest vibrates softly against mine as a rough, sexy growl erupts from his mouth.

"Sorry about that, darling. I got distracted by a beautiful girl in a red dress," he says in an accent I can't quite place. Scottish, maybe Irish.

"Do you use that line often?" I ask, raising my fleeky as fuck eyebrows.

His whole face lights up with a smile that could melt the panties off any woman, showing off two boyish dimples on either side of his mouth. Oh, he would have to have dimples, wouldn't he? They're like my kryptonite.

"That depends, did it work?" he replies. His voice is deep, yet melodic. *"Dat depends, did ih wurk?"* I shrug my shoulders in *you tell me*-fashion.

"So," he asks, his eyes never leaving mine. "Does the beautiful woman in the red dress have a name?"

I ease myself from his hold and turn to walk away. I look back at him over my shoulder; he is still standing in the same spot, staring at me.

"Isabella, but everyone calls me Ella." I shoot him a wink and try to do my best sexy walk over to the table where Cassie is observing the exchange. The amusement is blazing in her blue eyes.

Ella: 1
Hot Handsome Stranger: 0

Chapter Two

Cupids Arrow by Badly Bent

Cian

1 HATE VALENTINE'S DAY. It's just another stupid man-made holiday, constructed for poor love-sick bastards, but even this shitty Hallmark day can't bring my mood down. Want to know why?

We're in L.A. BABY!

It's hard to believe. We started out as just four normal Irish lads, with big dreams playing and making music in a garage. Now here we are, three days away from performing on the same fucking stage as the biggest band in the US — *Sinners*. We're heading on the road with them for the next six months as the opening act for their world tour.

Dad came through with that one; his old friend Rich pulled in a few favours with the band members and he scored us an audition. *Which we nailed. Thank you!*

Apparently, Sinners played a steady gig at Rich's bar, Jar's, back when nobody knew their names.

Then boom! One night... a producer from Limelight Records came in for a few drinks and signed them right there on the spot.

They owe Rich for their success, so they did him a solid and gave us a listen.

When Rich called Dad earlier today and found out we were in town, he asked if we could do a few songs tonight for his "Love Lock Night." Of course, we said yes. We owe the man everything after he got us an in for this world tour. Hell, I would've played at a kid's party if he wanted. The only problem is Rich suggested that we keep to the whole love theme because you know V-Day.

We will have to open with mostly covers, but Rich said we could throw in a few pieces of our own material throughout, hopefully, we can build some sort of American fan base. All it takes is one YouTube video and we could go viral.

The door of my hotel room, swings open with a resounding thud, indicating the arrival of one of my best friends and band members, Ciaran Maguire. "Helloooooo, Princess," he hollers.

I met Ciaran and his identical twin brother, Conor, when we were only kids through my little sister, Rosie.

When she overheard my best friend, Cillian, and I were setting up our own band; she persuaded me, to check out the duo at the school's Battle of The Bands contest. Thank god she did because they didn't disappoint. They blew us away with a badass rendition of Metallica's *Enter Sandman*.

Ciaran is one of the best drummers I've ever heard. I swear he can play anything and everything.

He's a musical prodigy, and to be honest, so is his brother.

Conor is an exceptional bass player. I realized there and then I wanted them in the band, and subsequently, 4Clover was born.

We have played a few gigs around Ireland and the U.K over the last few years. We built up a huge following back home, but this tour will hopefully get our name out there. *Worldwide*.

"You ready to go?" Ciaran asks before jumping back and sprawling out on the king-sized hotel bed.

"Yeah, two minutes. Let me just pack up my guitar. Where are Cillian and Conor?" I ask.

"They will meet us there. I need to get there early to set Sadie up," he says.

Sadie is Ciaran's drum kit. The only thing he'll ever love. Or, so he says. I beg to differ, Ciaran might be a man-whore of epic proportions, but his heart belongs to one girl and one girl only. Lily O'Shea. The fiery little redhead that is Cillian's baby sister. It's too bad for Ciaran she fucking hates him.

|***|

We arrive at Jar's Bar shortly after six. We finish setting up all the equipment just before dumb and dumber arrive.

"Where the hell have you two been?" Ciaran shouts from behind his kit.

Cillian ignores the question and walks straight for the bar. Not good!

I shoot Conor a look that says *Who pissed in his cornflakes?*

He must get the message because he replies, "He saw on Facebook that Rosie is out with Sean for Valentine's Day. He has been in a horrific mood ever since. Think he must be on his period or something."

I nod my head in understanding. Cillian is renowned for drowning his emotions in a bottle of whiskey. Looks like tonight is no exception.

Cillian O'Shea has it bad for my sister. He's been crazy about her for years, they've had their difficulties, life impeding their happiness, but anyone who knows them — would say they're endgame, even if they can't see that themselves. *Idiots.*

"Hello, boys. Here are your keys for tonight's Love Lock night. For the love of God, don't lose them." Following the voice, I look over to Conor. What I find is Rich practically naked.

I need to hold on to my stomach because I'm laughing so hard. This man, who is in his late forties, is wearing nothing but a fucking nappy and a pair of red wings.

"What the hell are you wearing, Rich? What're the keys for?" I ask between my laughter.

Rich walks straight over and smacks me on the side of the head. "Listen, boy. Stop your tethering. It's Valentine's Day, and I'm Cupid," he states holding his arms out wide like it's the most normal thing in the world to be walking around almost in the nip.

"These keys here are for all the males tonight. Every lady that walks in the door will get a lock.

The aim of the game is to find which girl your key belongs to. Simple," he explains.

"And the purpose of this is?" Cillian asks as he walks back from the bar, two glasses of amber liquid in his hands. He lifts one up to his mouth, knocking it back with ease. *Jesus, how is he not dead yet?*

"All in the name of love and fun, and you never know, you bunch might just find the one." He winks before walking over to the group that just came in the door.

"Yeah, the one who will suck my dick later," Ciaran snorts. Rich lets out a hearty laugh, showing he heard exactly what Ciaran said.

I set my guitar down and ask, "Anyone want anything from the bar? I'm going to grab a drink before we kick-off."

Conor and Ciaran both hold up their beer bottles and nod they're okay.

I pat Cillian on the shoulder. "What about you, man?"

"Jameson. Make it a double."

It's going to be a long night. Cillian is forever drinking away his problems, and if he is having Rosie troubles, things could get messy.

I make my way through the growing crowd towards the bar. I spot a few ladies over by the door, sending fuck me eyes in my direction. Maybe

I'll take one of them back to the hotel later.

Just as I pull my gaze from the leggy blonde in the tiny pink dress, a stunning brunette comes barrelling my way. She is far too busy trying not to spill the drinks she is holding to notice she will walk straight into me. I should move out of her way. She gets closer, and I forget all about moving. My god, she is gorgeous. Long brown hair that's flowing down her back, just reaching to the curve where her back meets her ass. She is wearing a tight red dress that moulds her every curve to pure perfection. My gaze travels downward, eyeing her toned, tanned legs, leading to the six-inch black heels that cover her feet. *She can keep those on.*

Before I can finish my assessment, she crashes right into me. *Shit!* The drinks she was holding go flying from her dainty hands, splashing all over my grey t-shirt and down the front of her sexy-as-hell dress.

"Hey! Watch where you are going, Ass... holy mother of all orgasms."

I try to hold back the laugh that's dying to escape me. I look down at the face of the little hurricane. Even in those killer heels, she only just about reaches my chest. When she lifts her face to glare at me, my heart all but stops. I thought she was gorgeous before, but I was wrong. This girl may be the most beautiful woman I've ever seen.

Almond-shaped hazel eyes with the longest set of black eyelashes, which nearly reach her brows. High cheekbones and the fullest set of bow-shaped lips painted in a shade of deep red. Holy fuck! I imagine all the things she could do with those lips.

I tighten my hold around her waist as she tries to pull away. I lower my head to just inches away from her mouth. "Sorry about that, darling. I got distracted by a beautiful girl in a red dress."

"Do you use that line often?" she asks. Her voice is full of sass.

"Depends. Did it work?" The smile that forms on her face is breath-taking, but it's the cheeky way she shrugs her shoulders that really gets me.

"So," I ask, my eyes never leaving hers. "Does the beautiful woman in the red dress have a name?"

She eases herself from my hold and turns on her heel to walk away. She takes a few steps towards a blonde who is looking at us, her eyes bulging out of her head. Just when I think I've blown it; she looks back over her shoulder.

"Isabella. But everyone calls me Ella." She shoots me a wink and continues to the table where her friend is sitting.

I stand there, just staring at her as she's walking away. Then I remember the key Rich gave me earlier. *Bingo. Please work!* "Ella," I call.

She turns on her heel to face me. She lifts her brow. With her hands on her hips, she waits for me to speak.

"Can I see if my key fits your lock?" *Well, that didn't sound creepy. Asshole!*

The sweetest sound I've ever fucking heard escapes her mouth. She throws her head back in laughter. My god, she is beautiful.

Once she gets her laughter under control, she replies, "As appealing as that sounds, I don't let random strangers I've just met stick their key into my lock, no matter how impressive it felt."

I raise my brow at her bold statement, biting the inside of my cheek to stop the laughter from escaping. *Does this girl have no filter?*

I reach into my back pocket, pulling out the small key, and with my free hand, I pick up the little lock hanging from her neck. "I mean this lock and key, but if you would rather the other kind, I'm sure we can arrange it," I say, as I give her my signature grin.

Her eyes widen, and her cheeks turn a pretty shade of pink with the new blush that's formed on them. I push back the few strands of hair that shade her face from view; I tuck them gently behind her ear. My fingers brush against her skin, igniting electricity between us. That's new.

"What do you think, darling? Can I put my key in your lock?" I say, with a smirk.

Another laugh leaves her gorgeous mouth before she nods her head. *Yes!*

Chapter Three

Crashed by Daughtry

Ella

I'm speechless. For the first time in my whole twenty-one-years of existence, I, Ella Andrews, am speechless! I open my mouth to reply and nothing comes out. *Not a single sound.*

I nod my head like one of those bobble head dogs. You know the ones you see in the rear window of some grandad's car.

After about what feels like an hour, my voice box decides she's not on vacation. "Yeah, sure, knock yourself out." *Really, Ella? Knock yourself out? Could I be anymore mentally challenged? Hello, hole, where are you? Now would be a fantastic time to swallow me up, thanks! Is he smirking? Oh my god, kill me now!*

He lifts the small key and ever so gently slides it into the lock. I close my eyes tight. I'm still not sure if I want the lock to open or not.

He places his free hand under my chin, tilting my face up towards his. "Don't close those beautiful eyes." Immediately, my eyes fly open and lock on his, his intense stare keeping me frozen in place.

He finally turns the key, the lock popping wide

open. The lock falls from the string around my neck, landing straight on the hardwood floor with a bang. "Well, would you look at that? Your key is a perfect fit for my lock." *Shut up, Ella! Just stop talking.*

He leans in closer, his mouth only inches from mine. He's going to kiss me.

Right before our lips meet, some guy in a 'Guns 'N' Roses' T-shirt pulls him backwards. *Seriously, dude? How rude.*

"Man, put it a-fucking-way, it's showtime," the rude guy states.

Mr. Orgasm looks back at the asshole that ruined my perfect movie moment. "I'm coming now, Ciaran. Give me a second."

Yeah, Ciaran. If you could just politely fuck off, that would be great.

He looks back at me with those amazing eyes. "Sorry, Ella. I need to go do some work, but will you wait till I finish up here? Please."

Shit! What do I say? I don't want him to think I'm some hussy that picks up one-night stands at a bar. Okay, time to pull up my big girl panties and play hard to get.

I place my hand on his rock-hard chest. "Maybe I will, or maybe I won't. You'll have to wait and see," I sass as I turn and walk away.

I stop in my tracks when his voice calls out from behind me.

"Cian."

I look back at him over my shoulder. "Excuse me?"

"My name," he explains. "It's Cian." With a smile, he turns and heads off into the crowd.

"What in the name of all that is holy was that? I could feel the sparks from all the way over here. That is one HOT man," Cas screeches from her side of the table when I finally take my seat.

Jesus, woman, calm your tits.

I go to answer her question, but the sound of a familiar voice echoes through the speakers positioned around the bar. My eyes travel towards the stage and there he is, standing front and centre. Cian.

He holds the microphone in his hand, looking every bit the Rockstar that his image portrays. I don't know about you, but there is something about a musician that just screams sex god, am I right?

I take in the other three band members. Guns 'N' Roses guy is perched behind the drums. His features are hard to make out from here, but his dark hair is pulled back in one of those sexy man buns.

He looks younger than Cian, but not by much. Standing next to Cian on the left is the bass player. Shoulder-length blond hair falls around his face. He is tall and lean in build, the muscles in his arms flexing with every movement.

On Cian's right is another guitarist, electric by the looks of it. He has the whole tall, dark, and broody thing down to a tee.

He is the mysterious one of the four-some. They are all gorgeous, the full rock god package, but there is something different about the singer that makes me weak in the knees. I know beautiful isn't a word used to describe someone of the male sex, but there is no other word to describe him. He is beautiful. His eyes finally lock on mine and he winks at me. *Cocky bastard!*

He pulls the microphone toward his lips and addresses the crowd. "Hello, L.A.! We are 4Clover. We have come all the way from the Green Isle of Ireland to kick off this Love Lock Night with a few songs. I hope you all enjoy. This first song is for a beautiful girl in a red dress. She came crashing into my life like a runaway train." His eyes find mine again. "Ella, this one is for you."

The opening bars of *Crashed* by Daughtry begins, and his raspy voice bleeds through the speakers, sending shivers through my body. I hold back the urge to squeal like a twelve-year-old girl at a One Direction concert. I am a grown woman, for Christ's sake!

The song ends, and Cassie's mouth is agape, her gaze focused solely on me. She is waiting for me to make a comment. *Not happening, missy!* "What?" I say, trying to downplay the little show that Cian just put on for me.

"What? That hot as fuck singer just sang the panties off you and every other female in this bar, and all you can say is 'what'?" she screams.

I shrug my shoulders at her. "I don't know. What do you want me to say?"

She levels me with a glare. "Start from the

beginning; leave nothing out. My single ass is living vigorously through you."

I tell her everything, from the moment I walked straight into Cian to the moment he stopped singing my new favourite song. It's safe to say that the song is going straight onto my iTunes account.

"So, should I wait around for him? Or leave and hope I see him again someday?" I ask, honestly torn on what to do.

"Honestly, Ella, if it was me, I would stay. You had a shitty day. You walked in on your asshole ex, licking out some hoe-bag's taco tunnel. Go enjoy yourself with Mr. Orgasm. If it leads somewhere, great. If not, you can always tell your grandkids about your wild night with a sexy musician. YOLO and all that. Let me put it this way: if it was me, would you tell me to stay?" she asks.

Hell YES!!

|***|

"Ella, what are you doing here? I didn't expect to see you out this evening." Jake asks after he approaches our table. There is no sign of thunder tits. Hopefully, she saw some sense.

"Ella, can you hear something? I swear it sounds just like a lying, cheating toe rag," Cassie questions, the sarcasm evident in her tone.

"Nobody asked you, Cassie. Stay out of it. What happened between me and Ella is none of your business," Jake argues back.

Cassie leaps from her stool, getting right up in Jakes' face. "That's where you're wrong if someone upsets my friend it becomes my business."

I step in between the two, pleading with my eyes for Cassie to relax. She must understand my silent message because she takes her seat without further protest.

Turning back to Jake, I cross my arms over my chest. I push the hurt he caused me back down, not allowing it to reach the surface. I know my worth, I will not allow him to break me.

"Listen, I don't know why you felt the need to come over here and make conversation. If you weren't already aware, we are finished. Where I go no longer concerns you. You lost the right to your opinion when you chose a side dish over the main course."

Cassie spits out her beer, unable to control her laughter.

Jake places his hand on my shoulder. "El, I'm sorry. It won't happen again. I've told Sandy already. It's over. I. Love. You."

Sandy. Arg, even her name is plastic.

"Don't care. I'm done with this conversation. I'm done with you. So, if you don't mind, I'm out with my friend and you're blocking my view." I say, pointing behind him to the stage where Cian is currently belting out Aerosmith.

Jake looks over his shoulder, his eyes following my finger. "Him, Ella, you can't be serious. He looks like he just escaped from prison."

"Bye, Jake," I intersect, not willing to listen to another word from his mouth.

He takes off in a huff, but it isn't long until I spot him again on the dance floor with Sandy wrapped around him. *What did I ever see in him?*

Cassie and I spend the rest of the night between the dancefloor and our table, just enjoying the night. I exchange a few glances with Cian throughout his set. Maybe if he plays his cards right, we can continue our earlier conversation when he's done.

Operation getting over Jake has begun.

Chapter Four

Bed of Roses by Bon Jovi

Cian

*W*ill this show ever end? The need to get off this stage is a first for me. I love to perform. The stage is my number one favourite place to be on earth, but for some reason, tonight I just want to be done. To get back to her. Ella.

The feelings stirring inside me are confusing. I just met this girl. Yet, there is something about her. She's captivating. Special. I have never chased a girl in my life, but I'm suddenly feeling like this might be the one I'd chase to the end of the earth and back again. *The end of the earth? Where did that come from?*

I shake those unsettling thoughts away and announce to the crowd, "Okay, Lovebirds, it's the last song of the night, so grab your someone special and head on over to the dance-floor."

Cillian begins the song with a killer guitar riff. I search the crowd for Ella. I find her just as my cue to start singing hits. I open my mouth and sing straight to her.

The crowd sings along when we reach the chorus of the Bon Jovi classic, but Ella — she is the only one

I see. She stands beside her table with her friend. They both dance and laugh. The way she moves is hypnotic. I watch her as she raises her hands above her head, swaying her hips to the sound of my voice.

The song finally ends, and I can't get off the stage fast enough. I say goodbye to the lads, and Cillian assures me he'll pack up all my shit.

I make my way over to where Ella stands with blondie. "Hey, you stayed," I say. Hopefully, she can't hear the excitement in my voice.

"Well, how could I not? After all, you sang that song for me," she smiles, shyly.

Her friend fake coughs from behind her, grabbing our attention.

Ella rolls her eyes and introduces me to her friend, Cassie. We take a seat at the table they have been sitting at most of the night; well before they danced that is.

"So, Cian, what's a bunch of Irish boys doing here, playing a gig in a small college bar in Los Angeles?" Cassie starts the interrogation. She tips her beer bottle towards her lips, awaiting my reply.

I let out a small laugh at her boldness; I have to give it to her; she wastes no time trying to suss me out. "Well Cassie, if you must know, we are in L.A., to support Sinners on their World Tour.

My dad is friends with the owner of this place, so when he heard we were in town earlier than originally planned, he asked could we help him out. We owed him after landing us the Sinners gig, so we said yes." My eyes wander towards Ella, "And aren't I glad we did," immediately her cheeks turn a pretty shade of pink as she blushes at those last words.

"Good answer, pretty boy," Cassie replies.

The conversation flows freely from there until finally, Cassie announces she is heading home. "As much as I'd love to sit here with you two love bugs all night, I have a threesome with Ben and Jerry I need to get to," she says with a cheeky wink.

I try hard not to choke on the beer in my mouth. *Did she just casually announce a Threesome?*

Ella must sense my amusement because she leans in close to my ear. "She means the ice cream," she whispers, humour lacing her voice.

Cassie whispers something into Ella's ear. When Ella nods her head in reply, Cassie waves goodbye before heading for the door, leaving me and Ella alone to finally get to know each other.

Ella

Have I lost my goddamn mind? I am walking across a dark carpark with a man I just met.

A handsome tattooed man, but still, he could be a murderer or a psychopath. *I highly doubt it, but it's a possibility.*

It might sound a little crazy, seeing as I just met Cian a few hours ago, but I'm not afraid. There is something about those stormy blue eyes that makes me feel safe, calm.

Calm. Find your calm, Ella.

Calm, that one little word. It makes me think of her, Nana. I hear her voice loud and clear, ringing in my head. Find your calm, Ella.

I miss her so much. She was the only person in this entire world I could depend on. After Mom died and Dad left, it was just me and her. Against the world. Now she's gone, and I'm all alone except for Cassie. Cas has become the only family I have.

I allow that particular memory of Nana to take me. I recall that conversation perfectly like it just happened yesterday. We were sitting on her porch swing when I asked, "Nana, do you believe in soulmates?"

She had her hand in my hair, gently stroking it while I lay my head on her lap. "I do baby girl, your grandfather, he was my other half. A part of me left with him the day he parted from this world."

"How will I know when I meet mine?" I asked her.

She was silent for a moment, mulling over her answer before she replied. "Well Ella, when you find the other half of your soul, you just know. Your heart might pound, the earth might stop spinning. Your knees might go weak, his touch might electrify your skin, but how you really know they are the one is when there is a complete sense of calm.

There will be no hesitation. No anxiety. No fear. Your soul will recognize him before you even do. So, my darling, never, ever, settle for anything less than that. Search for your calm. If I can give you any advice before I leave this earth, it is this: Find your calm, and when you do, do everything in your power to never let him go."

I try to hold in all the emotions that memory brings. That was one of the last conversations I ever had with her before cancer took her from me.

Cian's hand squeezes mine, bringing me out of my thoughts. He looks down at me with that gorgeous smile. "Do you fancy grabbing something to eat before I walk you home?" he asks, nervously rubbing the back of his neck.

"Emm, sure. There's a little diner just down the block; it's a 24hr so it should still be open." I suggest.

"Great, lead the way, Angel." He smiles, winking at me, showing off those delicious dimples.

Together we stroll hand in hand towards the little 50-style diner. Cas and I eat there as much as our student budget allows, the burgers are to die for and after those few beers, I'm starving.

When we reach our destination, Cian points to the large neon red sign, flashing above the door. "It's a sign."

"Yes, it is a sign, do you not have those in Ireland?" I sass sarcastically.

"Ha, funny little thing, aren't you? We have signs; it's an island, not the Stone Age. What I meant was the name is a sign, Maggie's. That's my Mam's name." God, I love his accent, so deep yet strangely lyrical. *Maggie's. Dat's me Ma's name.*

"Really. Must be fate." I wink, walking past him through the door he's now holding open.

We take a seat across from each other in the large corner booth, the silence between us more comfortable than awkward. Before we have time to read the menus, Maggie herself arrives to take our order.

"Hey kids, what can I get you?"

"What's good?" Cian questions, his eyes never leaving me.

"Can I choose for you?" I ask.

"Yeah. Sure, fire away."

Looking back at Maggie, I ask. "Can we have two bacon double cheeseburgers with chilli fries and two large strawberry milkshakes, please?"

"Coming right up," she places our docket on the table and heads towards the kitchen.

When my eyes land on Cian's face, I see a beaming smile, this one different from the one he gave me earlier.

"What?" I question.

"You eat," he states, sounding genuinely shocked.

"Course I do, did you think I got this ass from eating leaves?" I joke.

"I like you, Ella," he says, reaching across the table to push some loose strands of hair from my face.

"You're not so bad yourself, Irish," I respond the blush still covering my cheeks.

The food comes, and the conversation flows with ease. So far, it's been a great non-date. I grab a fry from his bowl — I've already eaten all mine — and continue with the next question.

"So, did you always want to be in a band? Or how did that happen?"

"Emm, honestly no. The band was Cillian's idea. He is a gifted musician and an even better lyricist, but he hates singing in front of a crowd. One day we were messing about and formed a band. I don't think either of us took it too seriously until we met the twins. That's when things got real and when people took notice."

"Hold on, explain to me, who is who? Ciaran is the drummer guy, right?"

"Yeah, and his twin brother Conor, he plays the bass," Cian adds.

"So that means, tall, dark, and broody is Cillian."

"Ha, yeah and I'm telling him you called him that," he laughs.

"So, you all have C names. Is that why you called the band 4Clover?" I ask before taking a sip from my milkshake.

"No, actually. There is this Irish legend that if you come across a four-leaf clover it will grant: Luck, Love, Faith and Hope, on those lucky enough to find one. We liked the idea behind 4Clover because those four things are all we ever need in this life. I suppose us all having C names fit too, so we ran with it," he explains.

Before we know it, two hours have passed. Conversation between us flowing like we knew each other our whole lives. So, when Cian asked me if I wanted to come back to his hotel? I didn't hesitate in saying yes.

I sent a quick text to Cas, letting her know I wouldn't be home, promising her I'd call if I needed.

Chapter Five

Show me Heaven by Maria McKee

Cian

We sat in that little diner for hours before making our way back to the hotel. I can't remember the last time I just sat and had an actual conversation with a girl. Maybe when I was like sixteen. We talked about everything. Ella is a dance major at UCLA. She is currently in her junior year. She talked all about how she dreams of dancing on Broadway someday.

Ella told me about her Nana, how she had raised her after Ella's mam died in a car crash when she was just two years old. I spoke all about my family and my little sister, Rosie. It was just so easy. I could have sat there until morning, just talking. I've met no one like her before. Not only is she beautiful. She is smart, driven, and has an amazing sense of humour. I could easily fall for her if I let myself.

We walk through the gardens leading to the hotel, and I pick Ella a red rose from a nearby bush. "Happy Valentine's Day," I say, playfully getting down on one knee before her.

"Thank you," she giggles sweetly before sniffing the flower she is now holding.

We fall into an easy silence as we walk through the lobby of my hotel. I can tell she is nervous. She has been twisting her hair the entire walk back, and she's already explained that she didn't normally do this kind of thing. *The whole one-night stands.* I will not lie, I've had my fair share of women over the years, it's all part of the parcel really, and honestly, I haven't found the right girl to settle down with yet. I know that when I do find her, all the sleeping around will come to a stop. I'm not a complete pig, my mam taught me to be a gentleman.

We make our way up to my room, and all the nervousness she was holding immediately disappears.

I kiss her lips softly. Then I pull her gaze up to meet mine.

"There's no pressure, El. If all you want to do is sleep, that's fine by me."

She replies by pulling me into another kiss. This one is a little deeper and rougher than the last.

I lift her up, and her legs instantly wrap around my waist. I push her up against the back of the door, giving me the freedom to roam my hand over her luscious body. I quickly lose myself in her, each kiss pushing me closer and closer to the edge.

Right here. Right now. I know I could kiss Ella forever. I've never really been one for kissing. It's too personal, too intimate, but with Ella, it feels different, necessary. I'm overwhelmed by how strong my feelings are for her, how intense just kissing her feels.

For the first time in my life, I want to slow down, cherish her, savour her, feel every moment, and let it consume me. Every taste of her leaves me wanting more. Each stroke, every brush of our tongues I commit into my memory, so I never have to forget these feelings she invokes in me.

Ella is like a drug. One I can already feel myself getting addicted to. I know I'm heading down a dangerous road. I can't get attached. I will only be in L.A. for three more days, then I'm off on a tour for six months. I can't help myself though. If being with Ella is playing with fire, consider me burned.

I slowly break the kiss. I trail my lips along her neck, making goosebumps erupt all along her skin. My hands slowly glide up her lengthy thighs under the silky material of her red dress. My hands find her ass, and I grab a hold of her cheeks, using the door as leverage to hold her up. I slowly tear the thin straps off her shoulder with my teeth. The front of her dress falls open, releasing two of the most beautiful breasts I've ever seen. Soft, round, pink, perfect.

"Cian." My name falls from her lips in a throaty moan. I slip her right nipple into my mouth, grazing the tip lightly with my teeth. Her back arches into me as she lets out a sweet, desperate cry.

"Please," she begs.

I set her back onto her feet and free her body

completely from her dress. The silk material pools on the floor around her feet. She steps forward. The sight of her standing before me in nothing but a red lace thong and heels nearly brings me to my knees.

"Bed, now," I growl.

She does exactly as I ask. Sinking to my knees on the floor beside her, I pull her hips to the edge of the bed and slowly roll the small scrap of lace down those glorious tanned legs. Her body squirms in anticipation. Once I have her completely naked before me, I lift her legs up to rest over my shoulders; burying my face in her sweet centre. I run my tongue slowly over her delicious nub, and her hips buck at my touch, enticing me further. *Holy Shit! I just found heaven between her thighs.*

Ella

OH MY GOD!!!!

I grip Cian's dark hair between my fingers as he works my clitoris with his tongue. I feel the familiar sensation of an orgasm building. I'm on a cliff.

So close to the edge, barely hanging on. Cian sucks my nub a little harder as he runs his fingers through my wetness.

He thrusts two fingers deep into my core, making me fall over the edge. "Oh, God." I cry out in pleasure as the orgasm completely takes over my body, leaving me quivering with the aftershock.

Before I know it, Cian is naked and climbing up onto the bed. His tattooed chest now on full display, and my god... *it's glorious.* The intricate designs that are woven up his strong arms and over his shoulder blades are delicious, making me want to run my tongue over every detailed line.

My gaze travels down his torso, my mind counting the ridges carved into his abdomen *two, four, six, eight.* Each one leads to the deep V that's like a beacon to his... *Oh my God, it's like the Holy Grail of penises. I don't know what I did in life to deserve this, but thank you, Jesus.*

"That was just the opening act, El. Now I'm going to make you sing," he says while positioning himself between my legs. He lowers his face towards mine, taking me in a possessive kiss.

"If you don't want this to go any further, stop me now because once I get inside you, I don't plan on stopping," he utters. His voice is lower, deeper than normal.

"Please, Cian." My words come out airy. My voice is still breathless from the orgasm.

"You will have to be a little more specific, angel," he responds with a grin.

"Please, fuck me, Cian."

That's all it takes. In one swift motion, he plunges into me with his long hard length. Thrust after thrust. Harder and harder.

A string of words leaves my mouth, but I am so far gone, I can't even comprehend what they are. My inner walls tighten around him as my climax builds.

He lifts my hips higher, allowing himself to

travel deeper into my core. Just when I think I can't take anymore, his movements quicken, and the look that takes over his face screams ecstasy.

"Fuck me, Ella, I'm gonna..." He buries himself inside me one last time, emptying himself into me and causing me to follow him over the ledge into the most intense orgasm I've ever had.

We both fall back against the mattress, our breathing heavy. "That was..." he starts.

"Amazing," I finish.

Cian pulls me against him, my back to his chest. He wraps his arms around my waist, engulfing me in his strong arms, making me feel like the most precious thing in his world. He places a small kiss right between my shoulder blades, resting his chin on top of my head. I've never felt so safe and loved in my entire life.

"Get some sleep, Angel. We can pick this back up in the morning," he whispers. It doesn't take long before my eyelids get heavy. Before I know it, I drift off into the best sleep I've had in years.

|***|

The morning sun shining through the crack of the hotel blinds wakes me from my deep sleep. I take a moment to recognize where I am. The events of last night flood my mind: Cian taking my body to new heights. I've never felt so satisfied. The smile on my face dims when I realize this was a one-time thing.

He told me he was leaving in a few days, so it

doesn't matter if the connection we shared last night was magnetic.

This will go nowhere, it can't. After a few minutes of admiring him as he sleeps, I come to the conclusion, it's better if I leave now before he wakes to avoid any awkwardness that might come with saying goodbye.

Slowly I remove myself from the bed, praying I don't wake him in the process. I quickly pull on my dress from last night, grabbing a pen and paper from the desk in the corner. I scribble a note thanking him for last night, leaving it on the locker beside his bed for him to find when he wakes.

Cian,

I'm sorry for bailing. Just know, last night was one of the best nights of my life. We both know that nothing could ever become of us, you're leaving for your tour soon, and I'm stuck here for college.

So, avoiding any awkward goodbyes, I thought it best I leave now. Have fun on tour and maybe someday, with a bit of luck, we'll meet again.

Thanks, so much for everything. I promise I will remember our time together for the rest of my life.

Go be the Rockstar you always dreamed of being.

All my Love
Ella xXx

"Goodbye, Irish," I whisper before tiptoeing out

the door.

6 Years Later

Chapter Six

Move Your Body by Sia

(Club Remix)

Cian

*L*os Angeles! I've been back here more than a few occasions over the years. Ciaran and Conor bought a penthouse apartment just outside of Beverly Hills back when the band first took off. We usually stay here whenever we have any 4Clover business on this side of the Atlantic.

This time, it's not business that has us frequenting The City of Angels. It is my soon to be brother-in-law's bachelor weekend. It's hard to believe that my little sister's wedding is in just a few weeks. She begged us all to play nice and show Sean a good time. Sean is a dickhead, to be honest, but if my sister is happy, I can at least pretend to be happy for her. So here we are in L.A., keeping Rosie happy and giving Sean a taste of 'The Rockstar

Lifestyle'.

As I stand in the shower, washing up before we hit Sunset Boulevard, I allow my mind to wander back to Valentine's Day 2013. It doesn't matter how many times I come back to L.A., every time I think of her. The little brunette that knocked me off my feet in one night.

I always wonder how she is. Did she finish college? Open her dance studio? Get married and have a bunch of little Ella's? That last one always hits me right in the gut. Ella Andrews will always be the girl who got away. The one night we spent together all those years ago embedded itself into my soul. I never understood how she affected me so much in such a short amount of time, but when I woke up in that hotel room alone, it devastated me. She didn't even leave her number.

All the women I've had after her, couldn't even begin to erase her from my memory. Trust me, there have been many, but not one compared to the beautiful girl in the red dress. I tried everything I could to get her out of my system.
I fucked my way through that first tour. Seeing nothing but her in all those faceless women. I wrote countless songs about her. I drank myself into a state for months on end, but somewhere in the back of my mind, she was there, telling me how disgusting my behaviour was.

After about a year of trying to rid her from my mind without success, I tried to find her. I contacted the university and apparently, Ella Andrews dropped out shortly before she was set to start her senior year. I tried finding her friend Cassie, but without a second name to go on, I got nowhere. I even tried social media and nothing. Not a trace. So, I took it as a sign to just leave it be. Let sleeping dogs lie, as my granny would say.

Even though locating her was an epic fail, I never stopped hoping one day, maybe we would cross paths again.

Pathetic, I know, but she was "The one that got away." The moment I saw her I knew she was different from the rest. Ella made me feel things I couldn't and still can't explain. There was something about her that made all logic fly out the window.

After my shower, I push all thoughts of her out of my head. I throw on a white button-down shirt and a pair of ripped jeans, gelling my hair in its signature messy style. I head down to the kitchen, where the guys are ready and waiting to hit the strip.

"Okay, Ladies, how do I look?" I make a show of doing a little turn for the group of lads who look like they've been drinking for the last several hours.

"A few more of these bad boys and I'd probably ride you." Conor holds up what looks like a shot of Tequila. He is laughing his ass off. It seems like I've got a lot of catching up to do. Everyone else is already three sheets to the wind.

"Where are we headed?" Sean asks like a giddy schoolgirl.

Ciaran walks around the kitchen island and places his arm around Sean's shoulder. "You, Sir, are in for a real treat. I've only booked us all a VIP table at The Doll House. It's the most elite gentlemen's club Sunset Boulevard has to offer. Welcome to the lifestyle of the rich and famous, my friend. Let's go see some tits," he announces before downing another shot.

|***|

We arrive at The Doll House just after nine. They have security greet us at the entrance, escorting us inside away from the growing fans that linger outside, waiting to glimpse the biggest band in the charts right now. I'm surprised to find this place is classy as fuck.

Ciaran really outdid himself this time. I was expecting some sleazy strip joint, not a nightclub. The bodyguard leads us through the crowds to the VIP section, where a stunning blonde greets us at the door.

"Welcome to TDH. My name is Opal, and I'll be your personal server tonight. Please follow me. I'll show you to your table."

Conor shoots me a look that says, "I'm totally tapping that." He slides in next to Opal, throwing his arm around her. "So, Opal, are you feeling okay? Because I think you're lacking in vitamin me."

She releases a high-pitched giggle before handing him her number. I don't know how he does it, but it works every time. □

Opal leads us through to a large dark room. There are strobe lights lighting up the dark space. A remix of *Move Your Body* by Sia is blasting through the surround system. In every corner of the room, there are cages hanging from the ceiling. Girls in sexy as fuck underwear dancing along to the heavy beat. It's not your typical strip club. It has more of a nightclub vibe. *More classy than trashy.*

When we reach our table, Opal informs us the main show starts in ten minutes. She takes our drinks order, telling us she will be back with them straight away.

"What the fuck is this, Ciaran? I thought you said there would be strippers," Sean states.

Is this guy for fucking real? He is marrying my sister in a few weeks and he's kicking off about the lack of strippers. Cillian gives him a death glare from across the table. Judging by the look in his eyes he is seconds away from losing his shit. I'm worried about him.

He's been falling off the bandwagon ever since he heard Rosie's getting married. Honestly, I was pretty shocked myself. I always thought when I finally got myself a brother-in-law, it would have been Cillian, not the douchebag that is Sean Morgan. The chap is a total bell-end; he looks completely out of place in his three-piece suit. He's out with Rockstar's, not the CEO of a Fortune 500. His blond hair is supporting a comb-over, and his face is cleanly shaven. He even looks like a total prick.

Cillian and Rosie have had their trials over the years, but anyone with two fucking eyes can see he thinks she hung the moon. I know this is the last place he wants to be. I can't imagine how I would react if the love of my life was marrying someone else. I'm surprised he came along at all. I sure as fuck wouldn't have.

The lights dim as the main show begins, and finally, we settle into our seats. Ciaran, Sean, and Conor throw bills around like paper planes while Cillian and I drown ourselves in a bottle of Jameson. Just a typical night out for the 4Clover boys.

Chapter Seven

Ella

I'm sitting in the makeshift dressing room of The Doll House, getting ready for tonight's show.

When I was a little girl, I had these big dreams of becoming a dancer. I dreamed of performing on stage, in front of thousands of people. I wanted to ignite feelings in them through the art of movement and music.

I guess the universe had a different plan for me because those dreams never once involved me dancing around half-naked for a bunch of pervy-ass men. Every night, I hang my dignity up at the door of this place, just so I can keep a roof over my head and food on the table. I'm not living my dreams. I'm living my worst nightmare.

I absolutely hate my job, but it's necessary at the moment. The only plus is the hours. They work well for me; also, the money is ten times better than what I'd get waitressing at some shitty dive bar.

Unfortunately for me, they're the only options I have. I'm not qualified for anything else, especially after I dropped out of college nearly six years ago.

I stare at the reflection looking back at me through the dressing room mirror. There is a girl, she resembles the one I used to be, but she's broken, defeated. Her face is thick with makeup — smoky grey eyeshadow, making her hazel eyes pop. Her lips are overdrawn, with a fire engine red lip pencil and matching gloss. Her long brown hair is backcombed to within an inch of its life. *Think Dolly Parton on steroids.*

Who are you? Where is the fun-loving girl you used to be? All answers lead back to him. I changed after that night. The old Ella left, leaving this imposter behind.

I try not to think about him anymore. It's been such a long time. It's hard though, especially when everywhere I go, I see his face. They plaster him all over every magazine, his voice blaring on every radio station.

I'm sure by now, he has forgotten all about the girl in the red dress. But no matter how hard I try; I can never forget him. He marked my soul that night. I tried everything to wipe his memory from my life and I can't. There is a part of me that will always belong to Cian Mulligan.

"Hey, girl," Sam sings as she enters the dressing area, snapping me from my thoughts.

Sam is one of the other dancers. She works with me here at TDH. The Doll House caters for L.A.'s finest. It's more "Burlesques meets Magic Mike" than it is a strip club, but nonetheless, it's still degrading.

All *'The Dolls'* are professional dancers; we perform sexy, yet classy routines all of which are choreographed to each individual dancer.

I met Sam a few years ago at an audition for a music video. We got talking, and she told me about this place. She had been struggling to find well-paid jobs, and this place made up the difference.

At the time, I desperately needed money. I had blown through all my savings, and it was hell just trying to make ends meet. She mentioned that TDH needed a new dancer, and she thought I should apply. I was working here the following week. That was four years ago.

Sam takes the seat beside me. She starts to fix her makeup. She has just finished her first set of the night, but she still has two more to go. "You will never guess who is sitting at the VIP table tonight."

Sam loves this game. Every night, there is some famous actor, singer, director at that table. We're in L.A. for Christ's sake. I'd be shocked if tonight was any different.

"Who? They better not be as tight as those fuckers last night; my mortgage is due next week. I could do with the extra tips," I reply.

Thanks to Nana leaving me her small bungalow just outside of the city, I own my home, but I'm struggling to keep it. There is not much left on the mortgage now, but if I miss a payment, the banks will be on my ass.

"Oh, sweetheart, I wouldn't worry about tips.

Those Irish men are throwing dollar bills around like yesterday's trash. You will be rolling in green before the night is through," she replies.

Alarm bells start ringing in my head. Irish men. *It couldn't be him. Could it?*

"Really? Who are they?"

Please don't say 4Clover.

"4Clover. Apparently, it's Cian Mulligan's sister's wedding in a few weeks. They're here for the bachelor party. Can you believe it? I love that band."

No, Sam, I cannot. *Shit! What the fuck, am I going to do? This cannot be happening. Out of all the places he could have gone, tonight he walks into the one place where I work. I think I'm going to be sick. Deep breaths, Ella. I can't go out there. What if he recognizes me? No, he won't. It's been six years.*

"Ella, honey, are you okay? You're looking a little green," Sam asks, her voice full of concern. I want to shout at her. *No, I'm not okay!* I don't though, instead, I flat out lie.

"Yeah, yeah, I'm fine. Just having a bit of a fangirl moment."

"I know the feeling; those men are HOT! Maybe I'll be able to persuade one of them to take me home for the night." She wiggles her eyebrows at me. When I don't respond, she places her hand on my forehead. "Are you sure you're okay?"

"Just tired, honestly I'm fine." *Oh, look, another lie.*

She gives me a quizzical look. She's not convinced. Neither am I if I'm being honest. How the hell am I meant to go out there?

Mike, the head bodyguard of all the dancers, sticks his head into the dressing room. "El, you're up in five." I give him a nod and say goodbye to Sam. "Wish me luck," I shout as I make my way to the back of the centre stage.

Okay, Ella, you can do this! With any luck, he won't remember you. It's only for four minutes. Then you can make like Usain and Bolt!

Four minutes. Four minutes.

Cian

"I would totally bend that Britney over a school desk," Sean pipes up, pointing at the busty blonde who is currently on the stage dancing to *Hit me baby, one more time.*

I'm this close to dropping that fucker into next week. That's if Cillian doesn't beat me to it. If looks could kill Sean would be ten feet under by now.

"I prefer brunette's," Cillian grunts in reply. It's the first time, he's opened his mouth all night. He's been sitting quietly. Too quietly if you ask me. Rosie is a brunette. That's why Cillian said what he said. Sean is getting to him. I can tell. Cillian is just moments away from knocking Sean's teeth out, and if it all kicks off, it won't be me stopping him.

The asshole deserves it. The few hours I've spent with Sean tonight only solidifies how much of a sleaze-ball he is. He doesn't deserve my baby sister. That much I'm certain of. You can guarantee, Rosie and I will be having a serious chat when I get back home.

"Give it up for our very own Britney," the house MC announces. "Now is the moment you gentlemen have all been waiting for; it's time for the lady of the hour. Raise your glasses, along with your wallets. Let's welcome to the stage, the one, the only, Miss Bella."

The opening bars, to *Buttons* by The Pussycat Dolls pumps through the speakers. The crowd erupts, and all the lights dim. A spotlight shines upon the stage. A brunette with her back to us is straddling the chair right beneath the bright glow.

All the hair on my arms stands to attention. My body hasn't reacted this way in years. Not since... *It can't be her!*

I focus all my attention on the dancer. She is fully covered, by a sheer black buttoned-down shirt, it reaches down to the top of her thigh-high black leather boots. When she turns to address the crowd, I search her face for signs of Ella, but she's wearing one of those masquerade masks, blocking her face from view.

Halfway through her routine, she pulls on her shirt, the buttons flying off in every direction. She tears off her shirt and swings it over her head, before throwing it right onto our table.

"Fuck me, she's hot," Ciaran shouts, his eyes never leaving the goddess in front of us.

Sean and Conor are now throwing bundles of notes all at once. I've got to give it to her, the girl can dance.

The next thing to go is her mask. She slowly unties the string, but she holds the mask in place. She takes two careful steps forward until she is standing right in front of me. She lowers her body down to my eye level.

Finally, she removes the mask from her face, throwing it right in my lap. My eyes lock with hers, and I feel all the air leave my lungs.

"Ella."

It's the only thing I manage to say. I'm shocked. What the fuck is she doing here? Does she remember me? I search her face for any recognition. *She knows.* She knows exactly who I am.

It's written all over her beautiful face. I stand up to touch her, but just before I reach her, she does the one thing she's good at. She turns and runs.

Chapter Eight

Ella

I run. I run straight off the stage and into the lady's restroom. I quickly lock myself inside the first cubicle. I take several deep breaths, desperately trying to gain some composure. What the hell was I thinking? I was so sure he wouldn't recognize me. Arrrg! I'm such an idiot.

As soon as his stormy eyes locked on mine, I knew. Cian remembered me. There was no doubt about it. The look on his handsome face would have been comical if I wasn't so freaked out. Then he reached for me, silently letting me know he never forgot. And what did I do? I ran. *Again.*

This is not good. I need to get out of here and fast. I don't want to see him. I can't. I've just got my life back together. My house is nearly paid off. Then I can go back to school, finish my degree, and get the fuck out of this job. I do not need the distraction that is Ireland's Bad Boy.

A loud bang comes as the bathroom door swings open. "Ella, I know you're in here. I saw you run in. Care to explain what the hell that all was about?"

Sam's voice echoes through the cubicle door.

"Nope," I answer, in a whisper.

"Well then, can you at least open the door, so I don't have to speak through it?" Her voice is sharp, showing off her annoyance.

I slowly pull the door open. I must look as bad as I feel because Sam's face immediately softens.

"Oh, honey, tell me what's wrong? It has something to do with those Irish boys, doesn't it? When I mentioned them earlier, you closed up like a clam."

I nod my head in a yes motion at her observation. *It has everything to do with just one of those Irish boys.*

I see the wheels as they turn in her head. Her mind running through possible scenarios. I can tell the exact moment she figures it all out. Her face suddenly pales, and her eyes widen in shock. She has put two and two together.

"Oh, Ella," she pulls me towards her. She wraps her arms around me, engrossing me in one of her warm hugs. My body melts into hers in defeat. "Which one?" She whispers into my hair.

"Cian," I mumble.

"Are you going to tell him?" she queries.

The tears stream down my face. I didn't think this day would ever come. For two whole years, I tried everything to contact Cian. I wrote letter after letter to his label. Begging, pleading, for him to contact me. I placed a countless amount of phone calls to his manager, leaving voicemail after voicemail. Each one left unanswered. I thought I had dealt with this. I was getting by. Sure, there were hard days, but I managed. I had to.

"I need. To. Get. Out. Of. Here," I get out between sobs. Panic wells in the pit of my stomach. My heart racing a million beats per second. I hate feeling like this, like everything is spiralling out of my control.

Sam takes my face between her hands. "It will be okay. Go home and get your head together. I'll handle Daryl. I'll tell him you weren't feeling well and that I'll be covering your sets. I'll have Opal get her hands on some contact details from Mr. Rockstar so you can reach him if needs be. Whatever you decide, I'll be here if you need me. You know that, right?"

I wipe the tears from my cheeks and tell Sam how much I appreciate all she's done for me. She saved me from a dark place all those years ago, and she just stopped me from losing it all over again tonight. I need to get home. I need to sort my head out. Then I need to contact Cian, do what will probably be the hardest thing I'll ever have to do in my entire life.

I make my way back to the dressing room to collect my things. Taking my phone from my bag, I quickly text Cassie, letting her know I'll be back early.

Ella: Hey, I'm on the way home. Explain when I get there. WINE NEEDED! Xx

Cassie: Kk, is everything okay? Shall I take out the ice-cream too?

Ella: I'm not sure, talk when I get home. Yes, to ice-cream. Luv you.

Cassie: K, drive safe. Luv u more. xXx

I pop my phone back into my bag, pull on my long overcoat and head for the carpark, before Daryl — my boss and owner of TDH — stops me.

Cian

It's been half an hour since she ran from me — a second time. Now, I'm waiting patiently in the carpark for her to leave. If I need to wait all night, I will. I left the guys to it.

I couldn't sit in there any longer. My mind races with questions. Why is she working there? What happened to all her dreams? I doubt this place was in her plans.

I've got to talk to her. I'm not budging until I do. Just then, I see a small curvy figure walk across the carpark. It's her.

"Ella," I shout after her. Her pace quickens. She's trying to avoid me, but I will not let her walk out of my life without trying to talk to her.

At least, not until she gives me an explanation.

I quicken my pace to catch up to her. "Ella, will you talk to me? Please."

She halts and spins on her heels. "What do you want me to say, Cian? We had a night of fun a few years ago, that's it. Nothing more to say."

"What do you mean, *nothing more to say*?" My voice drips with irritation. "You're working at a fucking strip club! What the hell happened to you dancing on Broadway or West-end?" I shout.

She takes a step towards me. If she was a cartoon character, there would be steam coming from her ears. "How dare you judge me for MY decisions?" She pokes me in the chest with her fingers. "I did what I had to do. I have bills to pay and a house to keep. We can't all be Rockstar's. I needed money, and dancing here was the only option I had. So, keep your opinions about it to yourself, asshole."

"You could have come to me. I would have helped," I state.

She throws her head back and fake laughs up into the night sky. "Yeah, hold on while I just look up a famous musician's number in the local directory. I can imagine how that conversation would have gone.

'Hello, I don't know if you remember me, but we slept together a while back, and I need money to pay my bills. Any chance of a lend?'

Get real, Cian. If I'm being honest here, I'm surprised you even remember that night. I'm just one girl who you bedded in what I'd say is a very long list. It's been six years; you don't owe me a thing. So, get off whatever high horse you rode in on."

I let out a breath. "You're right. It's been six years. But, contrary to what you believe, I never forgot about you. That night was one of the best nights of my life. I opened myself up to you in that diner; I told you things about me I've told no one. Yes, there has been a lot of girls in those years, but not one of them stuck. Do you want to know why? Because none of them ever lived up to the memory of you. Every girl that came into my life, I compared to you. You were the once in a lifetime, the girl who got away. When I woke up in that hotel room alone all those years ago, it changed me. It took me a long time to figure out why, and it was because when you left, my soul walked out that door with you. Ever since that night, it's been you. Every lyric of every song. You, it's always ever going to be you!"

I wrap my one arm around her waist while placing my fingers of the other under her chin. I tilt her head up to face mine. I see the internal battle she's fighting; it's written all over her face.

I can't stop myself from what I am about to do next. It's been far too long since I tasted her lips. I lean down and take her mouth against mine. She's hesitant for a second, but then ever so slowly, she finally kisses me back. The only thought I can form is *Home. Finally, home.*

Chapter Nine

Rockabye by Clean Bandit feat. Anne-Marie

Cian

*T*here have been many nights I've lain awake daydreaming about kissing Ella again. Now that it is finally happening, I get lost in it. God, I missed this feeling. I missed her. I know it's hard to believe; how could I possibly miss someone I hardly knew? I can't explain it. From the moment I met her, she meant something to me. I just haven't been given the chance to explore how much. *Yet.*

The daze I'm under breaks when Ella pushes me away. Her hands press against my chest. She takes a small step backwards, shattering the spell I was under.

"I can't. We have to stop," she breathes out, her voice low, just a pitch above a whisper.

I close the distance she's put between us, placing my hands on her forearms to keep her from bolting again. "Why?" I question. "Can you give me one good reason? If you can, I will walk away right now. Just one reason."

She opens her mouth but hesitates to speak. She locks her eyes on the ground and finally, she answers me. "I have a son." Her voice is quiet, but I can still hear the small quiver of nervousness that laces it.

Why does she think her having a kid would matter to me? It doesn't, unless she is married, or still with the father. I don't see a ring.

"That's not a good enough reason, El. Are you still with the kid's dad or something?"

She shakes her head, no. *Thank god.*

When I see the tears start to form in her hazel eyes, it devastates me. The last thing I wanted to do was make her cry.

"Please, don't cry, beautiful. Nothing in this world is worth your tears."

She looks up at me through her long lashes, her face paler than before. "I'm sorry Cian, I... I am... so sorry. I tried to... and... you and... I tried to..." The tears are now streaming down her face. The words fall from her mouth, but they're not making any sense.

I pull her into a hug, hoping to offer her some sort of comfort. Her arms immediately wrap around my torso as her body heaves in an attempt to control her tears. "Breathe. Take a deep breath, then tell me what's wrong," I say softly, unsure how to console her.

She does as I ask, but I wish I would have known that the next words to leave her mouth would stab me right in the chest. "He's... yours..." The words that fall from her mouth hit me like a fucking freight train. "My son... he's yours, Cian. He's our son," she explains between sobs.

What did she just say? All the air leaves my lungs, my body stiffing with shock.

My son, I have a son. I'm someone's dad. *My son. He's your son, Cian. He's our son.*

Suddenly I become dizzy. The echo of her words rings in my head, making my stomach twist into a ball of anxiety. Space, I need space. I take a few steps away from her, putting some distance between us. She's too close. I need to process this. Fuck, I have a kid.

How could she not have told me? This is definitely something I would want to know. I run my hands through my hair, trying desperately to process this news.

There are so many emotions coursing through me:

Anger. I'm so angry at her. Why the hell didn't she contact me?

Sadness. I've missed five and a half years of my little boy's life. Five years I can never get back.

Love. Love for someone I've never even met.

Happiness. I have a kid. I'm someone's dad.

That thought brings back the anger.

I look back at her, standing there gaging my reaction, a hint of sorrow displayed on her face.

"Why didn't you tell me?" I choke out. I need to know why she'd keep something so important from me.

"I did. I mean... I tried; I really did. I wrote letter after letter to your label. I phoned your manager and left dozens of voicemails.

Never once did anyone contact me back. I didn't have your number to contact you directly, but I did try. I swear." She takes a step forward, closing some of the distance I put between us.

Her eyes find mine. "I needed you. I was a twenty-one-year-old college student with no family, about to bring a baby into this world on my own. For months on end, I cried myself to sleep, wondering how I was going to manage. Eventually, I had to drop out of college and move into Nana's old house. I had enough money to do me a few months but, I quickly ran out."

She pulls at the long sleeves of her coat. Her shoulders lift, her body curling inward, showing her vulnerability.

"Cassie helped whenever she could, but she had school and a job. So, I had to take this shitty fucking job so I could work nights around Cassie's schedule. Nights were the only time she could look after him for me. She's the only person I have. She put her life on hold for me. She even moved in with us so she could watch the baby while I went to work. I owe her my life," she adds.

She steps closer, trying to comfort me by wrapping her arms around my waist, but I can't right now. I push her arms away, taking a step back. I see the hurt line her face. It kills me, but right now

I just can't be near her; this is too much.

"I'm sorry, Ella, but I need some space. I need time... to process this. I'm sorry, but you just flipped my world on its axis. You've just told me I have a son, and for years I knew nothing about him. I wasn't even aware he existed."

She nods her head in understanding. "Okay, Cian, that's fair, but here, take this." She reaches into her bag and pulls out what looks like a photograph and a pen. She flips the photograph around, so the image faces the ground. I try to make out what the photograph is, but I can't see it from this angle. She scribbles something on the back and holds it out for me to take. "Here. This is him. I took this photo of him last month, at the local park. It's one of my favourites."

I take the 4x6 photograph. I turn it around and stare at the face of the little boy, who is smiling wide back at me. My heart tightens in my chest. The tears well up in my eyes, and I become overwhelmed. A sense of pride follows through me. This is my boy.

"He looks just like you, you know," she states, pointing at the picture grasped in my hands. I'm still too caught up with the image of my son to reply.

Ella must sense my need to be alone because she pats me gently on the shoulder. "I have to go, but I wrote my address and number on the back for when you're ready to call. Regardless of what you think, Cian, I never tried to keep him from you. I did try; I did everything I could think of to get in contact with you. After a while, I just had to let it go." She places a small kiss on my cheek and turns to leave. "Goodbye, Cian. I hope I hear from you soon. Take whatever time you need to process this, but please, don't wait too long." She points back at the picture in my hand. "He gets bigger every day, and I'd hate for you to miss any more time. He needs you. He needs his dad." I'm still looking down at the little boy, who looks just like I did at that age, when a tear escapes me, the words she spoke making my chest ache. *My boy. My son.*

"Wait!" I shout after her as she walks away. Just before she gets into her car to leave, she twists around to face me. "What's his name? You never told me."

A small smile graces her saddened face. "Croí. It's Croí," she replies before getting into her car and driving off into the night.

I look down at the photo one more time before placing it safely in the left pocket of my shirt, right next to my heart.

I'm coming, buddy. Daddy's coming.

Croí. Mo Croí. *(My heart.)*

Chapter Ten

Hollywood by Lewis Capaldi

Ella

I sob, enormous fat ugly tears the entire drive home. They are uncontainable. My emotions are running ragged, my mind racing with so many outcomes.

Seeing Cian again, for the first time in six years, conjured up so many emotions.

Sorrow. Heartache. Resentment. Lust.

I spent many nights over the years, wide awake wondering, what I would say to Cian if I ever saw him again. I had just about come to terms with the fact it may never happen. Then there he was, right in front of me, spewing out his heart and soul.

His expression when I broke the news about Croí crushed me. Maybe I could have dealt with it better? Sat him down and eased him into it. I couldn't help it though; the burden of that secret has crippled me all these years. Cian needed to know. What he does with that information is out of my control. All I can do is wait now. I know he requires time and space to gather himself and his thoughts. Finding out you're about to become a parent isn't easy.

My mind drifts back, the memory taking me under.

I glare down at the two blue lines; the word underneath them stands out like a beacon. Pregnant. Those eight letters hold the power to change my life. Bile rises in my esophagus. I rush to the toilet, sinking to my knees, emptying the contents of my stomach into the porcelain bowl. I sit on the floor for what seems like hours, my eyes like sandpaper, dried up from all fallen tears. It's there, broken, my eyes inflamed, and curled up around the toilet, that Cassie finds me.

"Oh my God, are you ok? Why didn't you say you weren't feeling well? I would have come home."

I try to push the words out of my mouth, but they're caught on the tip of my tongue. I bury my face in my palms, my body shaking — from what, I don't know. Fear maybe. What the hell am I going to do? I can't look after a child; I can hardly take care of myself.

"Ella, you're scaring me, tell me what's wrong?" Cassie speaks softly, brushing her hand along my spine to offer me some comfort.

I point over to the little white stick that rests on the rim of the sink.

"Is that a..." Cassie starts, before cautiously walking over, and peering down at the small display window that carries my fate.

A small gasp leaves her, she rotates to face me, slumping onto the cold tiled floor beside me. Her delicate arms engulf me. Making me feel... less alone.

"It's okay," she confides. "Everything will be okay. I promise. I'm here. You won't be on your own. You have me, I'm here," she assures, caressing my hair as I break down on her lap.

A small tap against the driver's window pulls me back to the present.

"Hey is everything okay? You've been sitting in the driveway for twenty minutes, just staring into space," Cassie questions when I roll the window down.

"Yeah sorry, let's go inside. It's a long story. One I'm going to need a large glass of wine to tell," I explain.

Concern covers her face. I'm not a heavy drinker. Ever since I found out I was expecting Croí, my party days have been zero to none.

"How is Croí? Did he get to bed okay?" I ask as we walk up the narrow pathway, leading to the small veranda.

"He was as good as gold, like always. Why don't you go check on him and I'll grab the wine? Meet you back out on the swing in a few?"

"Sure."

I tiptoe my way down the short hallway leading to Croí's room; careful not to wake him, I gently push open, the bedroom door. There he is, my little man. He is sleeping peacefully, his iPod playing 4Clover songs on repeat. I never kept Croí from knowing who his dad is. Every night Cian's raspy voice plays through the small speaker, singing his son to sleep.

Croí's favourite song is; *If I ever*. Ironically, it's mine too.

> *"If I ever get the chance,*
> *to see that girl somehow,*
> *I'd hold her for a lifetime,*
> *chase away her doubt.*
> *If I ever find that girl,*
> *wherever she may be,*
> *I'd hold her for a lifetime,*
> *so, she can't run from me.*
> *If I ever get to see her beauty once again,*
> *I'd promise her forever,*
> *My love until the end."*

I tuck Croí in, wrapping him tight in his blanket. I lean down, whispering softly to his sleeping body. "I met your daddy tonight. I told him about you."

I gently push his hair off his forehead, giving myself a better view of his sleeping face. "Hopefully soon, he will come to meet you and see what a wonderful little boy you are. I love you to the moon and back. Sweet dreams."

After giving him a small kiss on the cheek, I switch on his night light and exit the room quietly.

I find Cassie curled up on the front porch swing, a glass of wine in one hand and a copy of 'Miss Mechanic' by Emma Hart, in the other.

She looks up from her book when she hears me walking across the creaky, wooden boards. "Okay time to tell me what's going on. You have me worried." She lifts her wineglass to her lips, taking a large mouthful while waiting on my reply.

I'm not sure how to put this, so I'm going to just get straight to the point. "Well as you know, I was at work tonight. I was just about to start my routine when Sam informed me that a certain Irish someone was sitting in the VIP section."

The mouthful of wine she has sprays from her mouth. "WHAT!!!... as in Mr. Orgasm, Rockstar, Baby Daddy... that, Irish someone?" the look on her face is one of complete shock, her eyes wide and her mouth nearly touching the ground.

"His name is Cian... and yes, THAT, Irish someone."

I launch into the whole ordeal, careful not to leave out any details. Cassie sits, listening intently, taking in everything. I don't know, what I would have done without her over the years. I come to the part where I drove away with tears streaming down my face. "... and here I am."

"Wow, okay, that was intense. So, what now, you just wait and hope he'll call?" she questions.

"Yeah... he will, I know it. You should have seen him Cas; it devastated him."

"Okay, if you say so, but whatever happens, you have got me. We have survived six years without him. What's a few more?" I know where she's coming from. She has seen all the damage that the years caused me. She doesn't want me to get my hopes up. She doesn't want me to get hurt, but I need to do this. Not for me, but for the little boy sleeping inside. He deserves the chance I never got; he deserves to know his dad.

I just hope Cian will feel the same.

Cian

After Ella drove away, I couldn't bear the thought of going back inside *The Doll House*. Instead, I order an Uber and try to call my sister while I wait on it to arrive. It's just after ten here, which means it's around six a.m. with Rosie.

I take a seat on a nearby curb, pulling my iPhone from my pocket. I search through my recent calls for Rosie's number. The foreign dial tone rings a few times before finally, she picks up.

"So, help me God, this better be good Cian. It's the butt crack of dawn," she greets.

I blow out a deep breath, unsure of how to approach the news of my newfound fatherhood. She must sense there is something wrong because her tone changes to a more serious one. "Cian, is everything okay? Did something happen?"

"Sorry for waking you, sis, but I needed someone to talk to," I reply, my voice low and full of sadness.

"That's okay, I'm listening," she offers.

"Do you remember a few years back? After that first tour with Sinners, I told you I met a girl in L.A.?" I question.

"Emm, yeah, vaguely, Ellie, or something. What about her?"

"Ella, Well, tonight, I bumped into her again. She told me I have a kid, Rosie. A little boy. His name is Croí."

"What! Cian, are you messing? Please tell me, you're joking," she shouts down the phone.

"I wish, she gave me a picture Ro, he looks just like me. I don't know what to do. She told me she tried to contact me through the label but got no reply. I was wondering could you and Lily check the records for me. Her name is Ella Andrews. There has to be some documentation in the system."

"Yeah, sure thing. I'll call Lil after this and get her to meet me at the office," she assures me.

"Alright, thanks Ro, I really appreciate it. My Uber is here, so I'm going to leave you to go. I'll call you when I get back to the apartment. Love you,"

"Love you back. Oh, and Cian..." she pauses.

"Yeah?"

"You will be a great Dad," she states, I can almost see the smile on her face.

My chest fills with pride at her words. *I-fucking-hope so.*

"Thanks, Ringa Rosie, Talk to you later."

"Bye."

Chapter Eleven

Cian

The next morning over breakfast, I sit the band down. I tell them all about Ella and the massive bomb that she dropped on me last night.

"Wait... so you're telling us you have a kid, with a stripper?" Ciaran's laughter is getting on my nerves. "Honestly, though, I thought if anyone would have a stripper baby, it would've been me. Not you," he coughs out between his laughter. *Why is he laughing? There is nothing funny about this situation.*

"Yes, I have a kid. And don't call her a stripper again, or I will set Lily on you," I threaten. Lily is Cillian's sister; the fiery little redhead is the only person on the planet that scares Ciaran Maguire.

Well, she pretty much terrifies all of us, but she *carries* Ciaran's balls around in her handbag.

"You wouldn't," he cringes in-between mouthfuls of his scrambled eggs.

I arch my brow. Try me, shithead!

"I'm not trying to be rude here, but can you be 100% sure he's actually yours?" Cillian's voice holds concern, and I don't blame him. If the roles were reversed, I'd be asking him the same question.

I take my wallet from my jeans pocket, opening it up. I pull out the photograph Ella gave me last night. I pass the picture to Cillian. I know the minute he lays his eyes on that little boy, any accusations of him, not being mine will disintegrate.

Cillian's eyes widen. "Holy shit, he looks exactly the way you did at that age. That's crazy, man." He passes the photo of Croí around the table. Each one has a similar reaction.

"He got your ugly mug. God help him."

"Two Cian's. God help the female population."

"Do you know his name?"

The last question comes from Conor, who hasn't really said much about the whole kid thing. He has his own reasons though, but that's a story for another day.

"Yeah, his name is Croí."

"Croí, as in the Irish word for heart?" Conor questions.

"Yeah,"

"That's pretty cool she gave him an Irish name, and a 'C' one at that. She obviously wanted him to have a part of you. He will fit right in with the rest of us. When do you get to meet him?" Cillian inquires.

I don't know how to answer Cillian's last question. Last night, I was so caught up in the news, I didn't get to ask Ella if and when I could meet him. I'm sure she wouldn't have told me about

Croí if she was planning on keeping him from me. I hope she doesn't. Now that I know about him, I'm prepared to do whatever it takes to have him in my life. My child will always come first, and nothing or nobody will change that.

"I'm going to call Ella after breakfast and figure out the details. I just needed some time to process it all. I spent half the night on and off the phone with Rosie. She gave me some good advice on how to handle things, and she's going to talk to Mam for me too. I think I might have to stay in L.A. for a bit longer than I originally planned, just until I figure all this out. I'll be home for the wedding, but I'll more than likely fly back here. I've already missed enough of his life. Time for me to grow up. I've got Croí to think about now," I explain.

"Take all the time you need. Everything else can go on the back burner. Your Dad will just have to wait till you're ready to announce the next tour. Croí is your priority now. All the 4Clover business can wait," Conor chimes.

|***|

I stand outside Ella's small cottage. The place is cute and dainty, just like her. There is a small veranda that runs the length of the house. Over to the right sits a two-seater porch swing. I remember back to when we sat in that small diner; she told me how she loved that swing. That night, she spoke about how she would just sit there, for hours with her Nana telling stories about, the good old days.

I run my sweaty palms over the dark denim of my jeans. I have never been so nervous in my whole adult life. I've played in some of the world's largest stadiums, with hundreds of thousands of people screaming my name, but compared to this, even that was a walk in the park.

What is the protocol for meeting your five-year-old son for the first time? Should I have brought him something? I'm so far out of my depth here. What if I disappoint him? What if I am a terrible dad? What if I fuck this up? All these questions are running on a loop through my head. I feel like I am going on an interview for the biggest job of my life.

I lift my shaky hand to ring the doorbell, but before I reach it, the door swings open. I freeze. Right there. Standing in front of me is my little boy. The words get stuck in my throat. My heart is beating a hundred miles a minute. I want to grab him and squeeze him tight.

It's right then, at that moment, I decide I'm never letting him go. I can't explain this feeling. Looking at him is like seeing my heart walking around outside my body. How did I make something so precious?

"Croí! What did I say about opening doors to strangers?" Ella shouts from the bottom of the hallway.

"It's not a stranger, Mom; it's my dad," he says, a proud grin lights his face, making his storm blue eyes glisten.

Dad. That one-syllable word makes me feel like I'm king of the fucking world. *That's right buddy, I'm your dad.*

"Well, are you going to stand there all day or are you coming in to see my room? Mom and Aunt Cassie painted it for me; it's super cool!"

Ella finally appears. She stands behind Croí, placing her hand protectively, on his shoulder. This is hard for her too. It's written all over her face. I can't even begin to imagine how she feels. I need to show her that I will protect them both with my life. I silently send her a message that says, *"I promise you. I won't fuck this up."* She gives me a small smile, gesturing for me to come in.

"Dad. Can I call you Dad? That was a silly question, sure I can. Do you wanna see my room?" he questions, bouncing from one foot to another. I see patience isn't his strong suit.

"Anything you want, kid. Absolutely anything," I express, ruffling his dark hair with my hand.

|***|

Three hours I've been here, sitting on the floor playing everything, from dinosaurs to transformers, just getting to know my son. I can honestly say, hand on heart, it has been the best three hours of my life.

Croí is a cool kid; he's so intelligent and creative. He reminds me so much of my younger self, especially the way he gets excited over the smallest of things. I can't believe I missed so much of his life though. I would do anything to get those years back.

Ella did such a good job raising him; he's such a happy little chap. You can see that he wants for nothing. I know Ella tried her best to reach me, but I can't help but feel robbed. I have so much I need to catch up on. Years of memories I can never remake.

"Can I show you my cuitar?" Croí asks.

"Do you mean your guitar, buddy?" Could this kid get any cuter?

"Yeah, that's what I said, dummy." He pulls out a small acoustic from under his bed. He is smiling widely, and I can't help but feel like he's trying to impress me. *That makes two of us, kid.* He sits on the bed and pats the space beside him for me to come and sit. I do as he asks, I've been following his lead all day, this is new for him too.

"Can you play me a song? Please, Dad." He looks up at me with stormy blue eyes. They are a mirror image of my own, and I know if he asked me to, I'd play him a million songs to keep that amazing smile on his cute little face.

I take the guitar from his hands and ruffle his jet-black hair. I start to strum the first chords of *Boy* by Lee Brice. Croí sways from side to side, clapping his hands excitedly, once I start to sing, he stills, his eyes wide, taking in every lyric. I recall the first time I heard this song. I remember thinking, if I ever have a son, I will play this for him every night. Now here I am, and I couldn't be happier.

I look up at Ella, who is standing, leaning against the bedroom doorway. She is watching me closely as I interact with our son. When I hit the chorus, I see a small tear escape her beautiful hazel eyes.

This right here, this is what I want, not just my son, but her too. My family. Together. Me, Ella, and Croí.

Chapter Twelve

Perfect by Ed Sheeran

Ella

I wipe away the tears that have gathered in the corner of my eyes. I lean against the doorframe just observing as Cian and Croí sit on the bed getting to know one another. Watching Cian play songs with our son pulls at all my heartstrings. The two of them together is a sight I thought I'd never see.

This is what I always wanted, for Croí to know his dad. I wanted them to have a bond that was unbreakable. The joy I feel at the sight before me is nothing short of magic. You would never even know they just met. It's like there's this invisible string that connects them. Two halves of the same whole.

Over the years, I tried to integrate Cian into Croí's life the best way I knew how. Through music. I played Cian's songs to Croí every day.

I got him a guitar when he said he wanted to be just like his daddy, playing music for the whole wide world. I never ever kept Cian a secret. Croí has known all about his dad from the word go. I told him how we met, how it just wasn't our time. Finally seeing the two of them together, both melts and breaks my heart. Cian missed so much. Deep down I can't help but feel like I am partly to blame for that. *Did I try hard enough to reach him? Could I have tried harder?*

Cian finishes the song, and Croí insists on another, jumping up and down excitedly on the bed.

"One more, then it's sleep. You've got to go to school in the morning," I interrupt, stepping into the room.

I hate breaking up their bonding time, I do, but it's already way past Croí's bedtime, and he will be like a demon tomorrow if he doesn't get his full eight hours.

"Why don't I sing this one for your Mam, buddy, what do you think?" Cian questions, a smug smile gracing his lips.

"Yeah, Dad, that's a great idea. My mommy always gets happy when she hears you sing," Croí replies, hanging me out to dry.

"Does she now?" Cian's smile turns into a full out grin, the same grin I fell for all those years ago. I shrug my shoulders silently in reply. *I have no idea what he's talking about.*

Cian's laughter fills the room. His eyes are on me, roaming over every inch of my body before locking into mine. When he begins playing one of my favourite songs, *Perfect* by Ed Sheeran, I nearly jump him then and there. If Croí wasn't in the room, I most definitely would.

I feel every single lyric. His raspy tone igniting a fire deep inside me, one I haven't felt the heat of in over six years. Each word of the song gives me hope that maybe one day, we could have a future.

From the first note to the last, Cian's eyes never leave mine, not once. Somehow, if it's even possible, I fall for him all over again.

|***|

We finally settle Croí into bed for the night after Cian reads him three different stories.

We make our way into the kitchen, and I offer Cian some tea in an awkward attempt at making conversation. Which he declines. I make one for myself, just to have something in my hands. Some sort of blocker to keep me from molesting the poor man.

I watch as he stands, leaning against the small kitchen island, his hands buried deep in his pockets. His shoulders are rounded, his body language telling me he is unsure of what to do. *That makes two of us.*

For too many moments we just stand there, looking at each other. Neither one of us knows what to say. I busy myself by taking small sips of my peppermint tea, hiding my face behind the giant cup.

Finally, Cian cuts through the silence. "Thanks for today, Ella. It really means the world to me. He's such a great kid. You should be proud of yourself. You've been doing an amazing job with him." I can feel the sincerity in his voice, filling my stomach with pride.

The next words leave my mouth before I can stop them. "How are we going to work this, Cian?" I know, maybe I should have started with some chitchat, but I need to know what he is thinking. He can't just walk in and out of Croí's life whenever he feels like it.

"Look, today was a great step, for both of you, and from what I can tell, you want to be part of his life, and so you should."

"I sense a but," he adds.

"But... I have to say this, your lifestyle isn't exactly easy. You're away half the year on a tour, and the other half you don't even live in this country."

I place the cup on the counter behind me and mirror his stance. He waits patiently for me to continue while I try to find the right words.

"I want you both to get to know each other. I do. I just don't want it to disappoint Croí if you don't show up. He's just a kid, and he needs stability and routine. It's my job as his mother to provide that for him. I need to know where he stands on your list of priorities. I don't want him to fall in love with you and then be destroyed if you decide he doesn't fit in with your Rockstar lifestyle."

Cian's face falls; he looks like I just stabbed him. I feel bad for hurting him, but it needs to be said. I can't let Croí fall in love with Cian if he doesn't plan on being a part of his life. Croí is all I have in this world. It's my job to make sure he doesn't get his hopes up or his heartbroken. If I'm being truthful, I don't want to get my own heart broke either.

The intensity in Cian's eyes as he pushes himself from the island to stand in front of me makes my ovaries scream with need. He takes precise steps, stopping only when he is towering over my small frame. He takes my face in his hands, cupping my cheeks. Those storm blue eyes lock on mine and I mentally fan myself. *Hold it together. Don't let his charm break you down.*

"Ella, I will do whatever it takes to keep Croí in my life. I've missed out on far too much as it is; from now on he is and always will be my top priority. I will be here any chance I can get. I will also fly you both to Dublin, anytime you want. Just ask and I will do it."

He pauses for a moment, his eyes scanning my face. I fight against the urge to lean forward just an inch and capture his lips with mine. *What is wrong with me? Why is he affecting me so much?*

The spell I'm under breaks when his deep melodic voice breaks the silence. "Maybe down the line, when you're ready, you might want to move there with me.

I don't know how to say this to you without sounding too forward, but I want it all. You. Croí. Us. We're a family. " *Dead, I swear, he just killed me with those words.* "There was never a doubt in my mind you were the one for me; from the moment I saw you, my heart was yours, and it always will be. Meeting you the first time was pure luck. The second time was divine intervention. We were meant to find each other. We were written in the stars. Call it whatever you want. Fight me if you feel you must, but I'm letting you know here and now, I am not going anywhere. I want you in my life, both of you. For now, and always. I'm all in, Ella. Mó chroí agus m'anam. My heart and my soul," he finishes by placing a small chaste kiss on my forehead.

I try desperately to stop the tears that fall from my eyes, but it's no use. Cian just said everything I wanted to hear. His words fill my heart with promise. I tell myself they're only words. I need to take this slow; it's not only my heart on the line here. I want to jump in headfirst, but I can't. Croí needs me to be rational, to think with my head, not my heart. I'm willing to try, but I need to set the pace. I can't just move us halfway across the world on some whim.

"I can't just uproot our lives here, but I'm willing to give it a shot. We will have to take things very slow Cian, for Croí's sake. We will take it day by day. One step at a time. It's going to be tough; your lifestyle is not one I am accustomed to, but if you're willing to try, so am I."

Cian runs his thumb across my lips. He leans forward and takes them in a passionate kiss. I'm handing this man the power to break my heart. I just pray to God he doesn't break it.

Chapter Thirteen

Cian

"I should probably go," I say hesitantly between kisses. Ella's taste is intoxicating, sweeter than the finest of strawberry wines. With each torturous stroke of our tongues, I get lost even further. I don't care though, getting lost in Ella has become an addiction. I can't think of anything else, but her.

Her taste infused with mine is like little droplets of heaven, wrapped up in the sweetest of sins.

I fight against the urge to wrap her legs around my waist and carry her to her bedroom. My body is aching with need; just for her. It's always for her. I need to stop before I can't. Ella needs to take things slow. She is still cautious. I will do anything to erase the doubt she is feeling. If that means I've to play by her rules for a while. I will.

Ella May Andrews is my last song. My last first kiss. She is the first and last girl to own me, heart and soul. I know deep down she is my forever. I just need to prove that to her.

Cillian was right; They're two types of women in

this world. The ones who hold your attention for the night and the ones who hold your soul for a lifetime. Ella is the latter.

I pull away from her slowly, kissing her one last time on the forehead. "I need to go before I do something other than kissing you. Can I come by tomorrow?" I ask in hope.

There is a slight pink blush highlighting her cheeks, making her look like the young woman I met all those years ago.

"Emm, yeah, of course. Croí is in school until early afternoon, but after that, it should be fine. I've to head to work at about eight though, so you won't have much time. Cassie will be home too but I'm sure she won't mind."

The mention of her job makes my blood run cold. I feel like I've been doused in a bucket of iced water. Possessiveness floods my veins. No woman of mine will work in a place like that. God knows I have enough money to support her. What does she need that dive for? The primal need to take care of her swirls around my body like a tornado. Logically I know it's too soon for me to demand her to quit, but right now, logic is out the window. *Mine, I take care of what's mine. She is mine.*

"I don't mean to sound all caveman here, but I will not allow the mother of my child to take her clothes off for money. I can't stand the thought of you in that place, stripping off for all those perverted men. It's not happening Ella."

I realize the minute the words escape my mouth

that it was the wrong thing to say. Ella is stubborn. She is strong and independent. The last thing she wants or needs from me is a Hulk-like reaction.

Her hands find her hips, her stance given off a hint of the sassy spitfire I once met. I pissed her off. *Shit!*

"Allow... Really Cian? You think you can waltz right back into my life and spout words like allow at me, and I'm just what?... To obey your commands like the good little possession you think I am. Not a fucking chance, Mister," she says, her tone putting me back in my place. "Oh, and that place you mentioned, the one with the perverted men... need I remind you, you were sitting in that place not even, twenty-four hours ago. Throwing money around and partying like it was nineteen-ninety-nine."

Just when I think she's finished tearing me a new asshole, she continues. "Get over yourself Cian. Just because you shit money doesn't mean the rest of us little people do. Don't think for a second just because you're back and trying to be a part of our lives, that I will let you support me financially. I'm not looking to be a kept woman. That's not what I am all about. I learned from a very young age how to depend on myself. I will continue to work there until I can find something better."

Abort, Abort. My mind is screaming at me to defuse this situation before it completely gets out of hand. I have no idea what to say though, not without putting my size twelve foot in it.

I close the space between us, taking her face

between my palms. I take a deep breath, hopefully clearing some of the tension that was residing in it. "Look at me, Angel." Her eyes lock on mine. The anger swirling in her hazel irises, softens.

"I'm sorry... I didn't mean to come across so possessive, but can you please try to understand where I am coming from. I just want what's best for you and Croí. I have no problem with you working, but you're better than that place. Look, maybe... you could just take some time off. Give us a chance to work all this out. If it's the money you're worried about. I owe you a lifetime of child support already. You can more than afford to take some holiday time. I don't want to fight with you, not tonight or ever for that matter."

I search her face for a sign, something to make me believe my words are working. "Can we just please table this conversation for a little while? Just until we figure things out. We can revisit it again in a few weeks. I'm all in Ella, and if you're in this with me, please, just let me help. For now, at least."

She closes her eyes, her eyebrows narrowing in thought. She huffs a breath out through her nostrils. She steps out of my reach, making me think I've totally blown it. When her eyes find mine again, a little spark of hope fills my stomach.

"Okay, I can take *some* time off... but don't think this conversation is over. I need to earn my own way. It's who I am." *Thank Christ she agreed. Otherwise, I'd probably have to take drastic measures — like buying The Doll House and firing her.*

I close the gap she put between us. I take her hands in mine, lacing our fingers together. "Thank you, I promise we will work through it, but if we are to make this work: we need to do it together. I appreciate that you're willing to take time off. I know this will take some adjusting on both sides, but we're a team now, El. You're not on your own anymore. You have me. I know I've said it already, but I will keep saying it until you believe me. I am not going anywhere," I promise her. I kiss her once more, sealing my promise with a kiss full of intentions.

When we finally break apart, I caress the side of her face. I gently tuck the loose strands of her long hair behind her ear while capturing her beauty into my mind so I can pull her image whenever we are apart.

"I'm going to go before I say fuck it and take you on this counter," I smirk.

"I could get behind that idea," she flirts, raising her brow in a come-hither gesture.

"Don't tempt me, you said you need slow, and right now, slow is the furthest thing I'm thinking. Goodnight, darling."

She insists on walking me to the door where we exchange a few more kisses. Neither of us wanting to stop. Eventually, I force myself from the porch, leaving my family behind.

As I walk down the narrow driveway, I look over my shoulder at Ella standing in the doorway, her arms folded across her chest.

"See you tomorrow, Angel," I shout.

"Tomorrow, Irish."

Chapter Fourteen

Ella

*A*fter Cian left last night, I hardly slept. My mind racing with *what if's*? So, this morning, I pulled out Croí's baby photos. I needed to remind myself of those years. As I sit looking through all the years Cian missed, old wounds open. In my hands, I hold every milestone, every birthday, Croí's first steps, his first day of school, each memory that Cian missed. It still hurts to think about how much I struggled all those years. I was so angry at Cian during the first few months. He was off living his dreams, while I put aside mine for dirty diapers and night feeding. I recall all the nights I cried myself to sleep, after hours of pacing the floors with a baby who was cutting his first teeth. I hated Cian, every time I saw him on a magazine cover, I wanted to punch his pretty face in.

I remember all the letters I sent, the hundreds of emails, I even offered DNA testing, but they all fell on deaf ears. Not a single word from him at all.

For years I thought he just didn't care, I assumed he was just ignoring me, but after seeing Cian's reaction, I realize now; he received nothing I sent.

He never heard the messages I left, begging, pleading for him to contact me. The way he immediately took to Croí surprised me. The way they interacted; you'd swear Cian never missed a second of his son's life. It was both heart-warming and heart-breaking; They lost so much time, I just hope Cian keeps his promise and shows up.

The chime of my doorbell pulls me from my memories. I close the album and place it back on the shelf. I rub my sweaty palms over the cotton material of my leggings. There is only one person I know, who could be at the door and I'm still not sure whether him being here is a good idea.

I pull open the door to find Cian — he looks his normal sexy-Rockstar self. It shouldn't be legal to look that good on a Monday. His jet-black hair is covered by a grey beanie, his eyes shaded by a pair of aviator sunglasses. He's wearing a tight black short-sleeved t-shirt that clings to his body, highlighting every single aspect of his ripped torso.

The way the material moulds against his broad shoulders does nothing to dull the growing urge I have to jump his bones. His bare tattooed arms are shoved into the pockets of his fitted grey tracksuit bottoms. They hang low on his hips, the band of his Armani boxers peeking over the waistline. I'm not ashamed of the way my body is reacting to him. The man oozes sex appeal. Once I finish mentally undressing him, I lock my eyes onto his. The glint in his stormy blue eyes, tells me he knows exactly where my mind went.

"Like what you see, Angel?" he teases with a sexy smirk.

"Don't flatter yourself, Irish," I quip, motioning for him to come in.

"I don't need to flatter myself; you're doing a stellar job doing that for me," he states as he follows me up to the kitchen from the narrow hallway. His words make my face turn redder than a stoplight. *Fuck you, hormones. Giving away all my secrets.*

We enter the small living room and instead of taking a seat, I stand fiddling with my hands, picking at the red nail polish on my fingernails. It's something I do when I get nervous and Cian makes me *extremely* nervous.

"What are you doing here? I thought you said you'd be here after three," I question genuinely surprised he is here so early. Croí's still in school.

"Honestly, I don't know. I spent most of the morning watching the clock. After a while, I just said fuck it. I wanted to see you. I *needed* to see you."

His words flatter me; I've also spent the morning with him running through my mind. The hands of the clock seemed like something froze them in time, each second like hours while I waited for him to arrive.

"I have to go out soon and collect Croí from school... I don't want to sound like a bitch, but could you wait here until I get back?" I ask, busying myself by fixing the throw cushions.

"It's only up the street. I'll be ten minutes tops. I don't want people asking questions. You don't exactly blend in with those tattoos." I continue with uncertainty. It's too soon to bring a famous Rockstar to school pick up. *I wouldn't want all the moms throwing themselves all over him. No thank you.*

"Yeah sure, I kind of figured it was too much too soon. I don't want to draw any media attention to Croí either... I brought some things to make us all lunch. It's out in the car. I can do that, while you go. I can have it ready when you get back, that is if you don't mind me hanging out here while you're gone," he offers, his voice displaying a hint of hesitation. I keep forgetting this is new to him, too. I can see he's trying to make an effort, which I admire.

"Yeah, that would be okay, lunch sounds amazing. It's been a long time since someone cooked for me. I won't be that long," I say. I grab my denim jacket from the back of the chair, pulling it over my t-shirt. "Do you need help to bring in the groceries before I leave?" I offer.

"No, it's fine, I've got them," he steps closer, closing the distance between us. He lifts his hand to my cheek, his fingers brushing back the loose strands of hair that have escaped my signature mom-bun. He tucks them behind my ear, a shiver runs through me at his soft touch. "You look beautiful today," he smiles at me, his blue eyes lighting up his face.

I lick my lips, swallowing back the lump in my throat. The way he is looking at me is intense, but I'm quickly learning that is part of Cian's personality. From the little I've seen of him since we met again, Cian is an all-or-nothing kind of guy. He jumps in with both feet. He isn't afraid of the fall. He just trusts he'll land where he's meant to and somehow, I find that highly attractive.

We stand there for a moment, just staring into each other's eyes. The sexual tension between us ready to combust. "I better go?" I say, those three words coming out more like a question than a statement.

"You don't sound so sure of that sweetheart," he chuckles. The raspy sound hitting me right in my core.

"I have to go."

"Better," he winks. Cian leans forward brushing his perfect lips over mine in a feather-light touch. "Go, get our boy. I'll be right here waiting when you get back," he whispers against my lips.

I close my eyes; I take a deep breath. His masculine scent fills my nostrils, a smell that is distinctly him. I step backwards, removing myself from his hold. "See you soon."

"See you soon," he repeats

|***|

I open the door to my humble home. Croí rushes past me straight into his dad's arms. "Dad you came back," he says with excitement. Those four words squeeze my heart, I love that he is enjoying his dad being here, but it also scares me how quickly he is getting attached — what if this doesn't last?

"Of course, I did, buddy. There's nowhere in the world I'd rather be," Cian tells him, rustling his hair with his tattooed hands. "Are you hungry? I made lunch."

"I'm starving. My brain used all my food. I had a spelling test; I got ten out of ten. I'm a genius," Croí launches into his day, while Cian picks him up, listening to every word intently. They head into the kitchen as I stand to observe them together. It really is a sight. Nothing beats the sight of a sexy man loving on his kid.

I follow behind them, entering the kitchen. The first thing to hit me is the amazing smell of creamy mushroom soup. Croí's perched on the stool, already stuffing his face. "Wow, this smells amazing. How did you make all this so quickly?"

"I made it this morning before I came. I just needed to heat it up. I also made some ham and cheese toasties too, or do you yanks call them grilled ham and cheese?" Cian teases, holding out the stool for me to sit before placing the soup and a sandwich in front of me.

"You're hilarious, Irish. But yanks are from New York, not Cali. Keep it up and I will pack up your toasties and you can eat them in your car... by yourself," I sass back with a cheeky wink making him laugh. "Your words wound me, Angel," he mocks, holding his hand to his chest.

"What's a yank?" Croí asks, his mouth full of cheese causing Cian to spit out the mouthful of coffee he just took.

"Never mind, what did I tell you about talking with your mouth full?" I avert his question.

"Sorry, Mom."

This, I could get used to. Us, together, playing happy family. I'm still cautious though, I barely know Cian. I let my gaze flick between the two of them and I know I want this, but don't all good things end? I can't see how we can make this work. I'm scared it won't. If Cian decides we don't fit into his Rockstar lifestyle, it will leave Croí and I in pieces. I wouldn't know how to put us back together again if that happens.

Cian must have sensed my internal battle because he moves to stand behind me, wrapping his arms around my waist and resting his head on my shoulder. "Stop overthinking this, Angel. I promise this is not temporary. I'm here and I'm not going anywhere," he whispers against my neck, making my skin break out in goosebumps.

"I'm all in, baby," he adds, placing a gentle kiss behind my ear.

God, I hope so.

Chapter Fifteen

Drive By by Train

Ella

*T*he afternoon passes by in a blink of an eye.

Croí is besotted by his dad. They've spent the last hour running around the house shooting each other with Nerf guns. I don't think I've ever heard my son laugh as much as he did today. Cian is good for him. It always worries me that Croí doesn't have a good male role model. Cassie and I do our best, but there are still times I can't help but think − He needs a father figure in his life, someone he can look up to. I'm glad he is getting that now.

I stand washing up the plates we used at dinner, the small portable radio beside the sink playing *Drive By*, by Train. I hum along to the melody, my head bopping to the beat and my foot tapping by its own accord.

Two strong arm's grip my hips, spinning me away from the sink and pulling me closer to a toned hard chest. I look up meeting a pair of stormy blue eyes. "Didn't I tell you I'd look after that, Angel?" Cian questions, still swaying my hips to the music with his hands.

"It's only a few things. Besides, you made lunch and bought us dinner, I don't expect you to clean up too," I offer. I reach up with my soap-filled hands, grabbing hold of his handsome face I smear the suds all over his cheeks. I struggle to contain my laughter. When Cian's sexy mouth flashes me a million-dollar grin, the laughter erupts like a volcano.

"You just ruined our moment with your shenanigans," he chuckles, twirling me around in an attempt at dancing. He steps us back against the sink. Before I realize what, he is doing, he scoops up a hand full of suds blowing the bubbles into my face.

"Oh, that's it, Rockstar, you're going down." I threaten, poking him playfully in the chest.

Before I can follow through with my attack, he lifts me off my feet flinging me over his shoulder like I weigh nothing. "Put me down," I screech, pounding my fists against his back. "Cian!"

He sings the chorus of the Train song with ease, his body vibrating beneath me as he chuckles at my protests.

"Croí, buddy, I need your help. There's a crazy lady on my back," he shouts into the living room, where Croí is busy playing with his Lego.

Croí rams through the door with a Nerf machine gun, he pulls the trigger shooting me in the ass with spongy orange and blue bullets.

"Oh my God, you little minion, whose side are you on?" I shout.

Both are now laughing their heads off. Cian puts me down and runs from the kitchen with Croí on his heels. I can't help but wish, we could stay this way forever; Happy and not a care in the world.

|***|

"Hey, Mama. Did I miss Mr. Orgasmic? I was hoping to get a glimpse of his fine ass before he left," Cassie greets me as she takes a seat on the armchair across from the couch I'm curled upon.

"No, he's still here. He's putting Croí to bed. How was work?" I ask, trying hard to suppress the smile that's been on my face all day.

Cassie arches her brow, silently calling me out on my good mood. "It's good to see you smiling again," she points out. "Work was good, I'm just tired of all the wedding shoots. I need more action." She kneels forward to unzip her knee-high boots, pulling them off with a heavy sigh. "Do you think Rockstar needs a photographer for their next tour? I could snap picture after picture of those boys all day, without complaining," she adds, making me giggle.

"So, how did things go around here?" She asks, looking around the now turned upside down living room. "Judging from your face alone... I'd guess pretty well," she says in a hushed tone, so Cian won't hear us from Croí's room.

"Cas, it was great. I've not had that much fun in a long time, Cian is fantastic with Croí."

"Why am I sensing some hesitation?" she

questions, pulling her feet beneath her.

"I don't know, I can feel myself falling for him already and it's only been two days. I can't help it, seeing how good he is with Croí does things to me. It's so hard not to want more with him, he is pretty amazing," I explain. I sit up from the couch, turning to face her.

"What are you so scared of?" she asks her face softening with concern.

"What if he leaves, Cassie? I know he said he wouldn't... but can I risk it?"

"Sweetheart, you can't live your life based on *what ifs?*" She offers. "That doesn't mean you have to jump right in either. Just take it slow, let his actions speak louder than his words. At the end of the day, he'll still be Croí's dad. He will always be in your life, regardless."

"I know," I answer, putting my head into my palms. I stand up from the couch, wiping my palms against my mom jeans. "I'm going to say goodnight to Croí."

She stands to join me.

"Where are you going?" I question, normally, you've to drag Cas of the couch after one of her shoots.

"If you think I'm passing up the opportunity of seeing *Mr. Baby Daddy* in action, you are sadly mistaking my friend," she taps my bum playfully. "Lead the way, Ella. My loins are aching just thinking about it."

I laugh at her open fascination with Cian. She's a

sucker for a sexy musician. She once ran into my room at four in the morning because TMZ had posted a photo of Atticus Walker in a pair of pink swim shorts. *I kid you not.*

We tiptoe down the small hallway, hoping to sneak a little glance before they notice us. I'm not prepared for the sight we find. *Someone, call 911, my ovaries just spontaneously combusted.*

"There is a God," Cassie whispers from over my shoulder.

"Ssshhh, you'll wake them." I scold her through my teeth, keeping my voice barely above a whisper.

"Be right back," she rushes out, taking off down the hall towards the sitting room.

I lean against the door frame taking it all in. Cian's large frame is squeezed into Croí's tiny bed. He lays flat on his back. His left arm bent at the elbow and tucked under his head. His right arm's wrapped tightly around Croí — who has *his* head nestled against Cian's chest. Cian has his face buried into Croí's hair. The book they were reading lays open on the floor. In all my life, I've seen nothing so heart-warming.

Click, click, click.

I turn to find Cassie snapping picture after picture of Cian and Croí as they sleep soundly.

"What are you doing?" I ask, knowing full well I will beg her for several copies of each shot.

"I'm documenting," she winks. "This is a moment worth remembering."

Click, click, click.

"Give me that damn camera." I hold out my hand, urging her to hand it over.

"Never," she replies, pulling it tightly to her chest. "My precious," she adds, taking off towards her room while laughing her ass off. *Unbelievable.*

I take another look at Cian with Croí, debating with myself whether I should wake him. He looks so peaceful. I decide to leave him for a little while, at least until I've finished tidying up the mess, we made in the living room earlier.

I flick off the main light and switch on the small *Bumblebee Transformer* night-light beside the bed. Once I've placed a blanket over them both, I head to the living room to clean up. I need to keep my mind busy from the thoughts of Cian and his new role in our lives. Cassie's words from earlier tonight, ring through my mind. *"Just take it slow, let his actions speak louder than his words."*

How do I take it slow when my heart beats a million beats a minute, every time I see him loving our son? How fast is too fast?

|***|

After I clean the entire house, I fill myself a glass of wine and head out to the porch swing. Cian is still sleeping, and I don't have the heart to wake him. So instead, I go where I always do when my mind is restless. Nana's swing. It's where I used to sit with her and talk things over. Since she passed, I sit here and talk to the stars. I hope that wherever she is — she's listening.

I lift my glass in cheers to the sky before taking a sip of my Malbec. I huff out a heavy sigh, blowing away the emotions that came with today.

"He's back," I offer to the stars. "What am I meant to do?" I pause, waiting for an answer I know isn't coming.

I twirl the wine inside the glass. "Can you at least give me some sort of sign, am I doing the right thing letting him be a part of our lives after so long?" *Silence.*

"Thanks for the advice, I appreciate it," I say sarcastically, knocking back the rest of my wine like a tequila shot.

"Hey, what're you doin' out here?" A masculine voice speaks from the doorway. I don't need to look to see who it is. I'd know that accent anywhere. Yet, even so, my eyes move in his direction.

"Just thinking," I move over, and pat the space beside me — a silent invitation for him to join me. He closes the distance and sits down, his leg brushing against mine.

"I'm sorry for falling asleep. I didn't realize how tired I was. It's been a crazy few days," he apologizes, running his right hand through his hair. *Dude, you really need to stop doing that; it's highly distracting.*

"No worries, having a kid is tiring, trust me I've had one for years," I say, bumping him with my shoulder to show my sarcasm. "The tiredness never leaves you. Most days I walk around like an exhausted Pidgeon."

He forces out a small laugh, but I can hear the regret that laces it. "What's wrong, Irish?"

He takes the wine glass from my hand, placing it on the small coffee table to the side. He turns back to face me, grabbing my attention with the intensity in his eyes. "I'm sorry, Ella. I'm so sorry you had to do those early years by yourself. You've got to believe me when I say: If I had of known about Croí, I would have been here. You shouldn't have had to do all that alone."

"I wasn't by myself, I had Cassie, and please stop apologizing it wasn't your fault either," I assure him.

"I know, but I still feel guilty."

He wraps his arm around my shoulder, pulling me closer to his chest. "I'm going to make it up to you both, I promise."

He places a small kiss on my forehead, then my nose and finally his lips meet mine. Our tongues intertwine and I've to suppress the urge to moan into his mouth. All too quickly he pulls away, leaving me wanting more.

His eyes search my face — for what I have no idea. "I'm going to go. Can I come by tomorrow?" He questions.

I nod my head. *Yes.*

He stands to leave, and this sensation arises in the pit of my stomach. I realize what it is immediately. *I don't want him to go.* I push that thought away. It is far too soon for an impromptu sleepover. Slow, I need slow.

I push myself up off the swing and step into his open arms. He rests his head atop of mine. "Goodnight, Angel," he whispers into my hair.

"Goodnight, Irish."

He turns to leave, and I internally kick myself for letting him go.

Tomorrow.

Chapter Sixteen

I Can't Help Falling in Love with You by Elvis Presley

Cian

"What time are you flying out at?" I question Cillian.

I shovel down my breakfast. The rest of the boys flew back home last week, but Cillian stayed on for an extra few days; he said he needed to clear his head.

"I leave here in an hour; the flight is at ten. Are you sure you're not coming?" he asks. He looks like shit, his head resting against the counter.

"Yeah, I'm sure, I want to spend as much time as I can with Croí before I have to head back for my brotherly wedding duties."

Cillian mutters something inaudible under his breath.

"What?"

He lifts his head, looking me dead in the eye. "What does Rosie see in him, Cian? Seriously, can you tell me? Because I'm at a fucking loss here!"

I hate seeing him like this. I try not to get involved in whatever is going on with him and my sister; it's not my business. Since her engagement party to Sean, Cillian hasn't been doing so great. I make a mental note to call Ciaran, get him to check in on him while I'm still here. □"I don't know, mate. If it's any consolation, I wish she chose you," I offer.

Cillian stands, running his hands through his brown hair. The sadness behind his green eyes guts me. He is my best friend, and he is hurting, but Rosie's my sister, and I've to respect whatever decision she makes. And if that's Sean... I've to support that, even if he is a total wanker.

"Yeah, well, she didn't. She chose someone who has no respect for her; he treats her like dirt, Cian. I don't think I can go to that wedding. I can't sit there and watch her walk down the aisle into the arms of someone else," he explains.

Ella's face flashes through my mind. Could I watch her marry someone else? The answer hits me harder than a wrecking ball. I know there and then; I'll do whatever it takes to make her fall in love with me the way I'm falling for her. I'm already up the creek without a paddle. If I'm being honest, I don't even have a boat... I'm swimming in the deep end, praying I'm strong enough to make it through the current.

It's been ten days since they came back into my life and already, I can't see a day without them. I've been spending every spare minute getting to know them both, just doing normal everyday stuff — like cooking meals and playing house. Things between Ella and me have been painfully slow, nothing more than a few kisses and innocent touches, but I'm hoping tonight that will change. Tonight, I'm taking her on our first official date. Cassie offered to babysit so I'm taking full advantage of it. I want to convince Ella to come home to Ireland with me. Even for the wedding, I want her to meet my family. I want Croí to meet *his* family.

"Are you even listening to me?" Cillian moans.

"Yeah, sorry... Have you tried talking to her?"

"I'm done trying, I can't keep fighting for someone who doesn't want saving." His head hangs in defeat, and I stand to grab him in a half-man hug, patting him on the back. "I'm sorry. I wish I could help, but you know Rosie better than I do. She's stubborn and once she's made up her mind... There's no changing it."

"I know, but there is something in the pit of my stomach telling me there is more to it. I just don't know what. I'm sorry for loading all this on you. You have enough going on with your ready-made family," he jokes, brushing off his rotten mood. "I'm going to go pack. I'll see you when you get back. Say hello to little Croí for me," he adds before turning to leave the room.

"Will do. I'll call you during the week," I shout after him. He raises his hand, waving goodbye and flipping me off in the process.

Time to plan the best date Ella has ever been on.

Ella

Why the hell am I so nervous? I'm going on a date with the father of my child, for the love of God. My clothes are thrown all around my bedroom. *Is that a thong stuck to the light shade? Oh... for fuck's sake!*

All around me, shoes litter the floor. *That's it, I'm not going... I've nothing to wear; unless you count mom jeans and an off-white t-shirt. Nothing screams sexy like a five-year-old t-shirt.*

It's been almost two weeks since Cian landed back into my life. Things have been going amazing. He is fantastic with Croí.

They really hit it off. If I'm honest, I am kind of jealous because now I am the one who feels like an outcast.

Croí idolizes his dad, mirroring his every move. He is no longer Momma's boy, and selfishly, that makes me a little sad. Every day, Cian comes by to help me with Croí, but once the little man is tucked in tight, Cian leaves. He kisses me goodbye, leaving me craving for more.

Hopefully, tonight that will change. I can't take it anymore. Every time he touches me, electricity sparks between us. My body is desperate for release. Being around him is killing me. I need more than PG13. *I want X-fucking-Rated. Fifty shades of orgasms, please.*

I know it was my idea to take things slow, but my God, I didn't mean for him to come to a complete standstill. A girl has needs. There is only so much BOB can do. *For those of you wondering, BOB is my Battery-Operated-Boyfriend.*

"Wow! What the hell happened here?" Cassie asks, her eyes darting around my room. I'm not a messy person but right now, my room looks like it's been robbed.

Why can't I look like her? Even in her yoga pants, she looks amazing. Life is so unfair.

"I'm freaking out, Cian will be here in an hour, and my bedroom looks like Gap on Black Friday. What do you wear on a date with a Rockstar?"

Cassie rushes from the room, leaving me standing there in confusion. *Okay then, thanks for the help!* She returns seconds later, holding up a red dress. There's a smugness lining her lips. It takes me a second to realize why. *Oh, my god! Where did she get that?*

"Is that...?" I thought I threw that dress away years ago. It reminded me of him; every time I opened the closet it would mock me.

"Oh, yes." She wiggles her perfectly plucked eyebrows. "It's *THE* dress. The one that brought the famous Rockstar Cian Mulligan to his knees all those years ago." She holds it out, and I snatch it from her grip. I pull the dress over my head with ease. Someone must be looking down on me because it's still a perfect fit. *Got to love a good bodycon.*

I loved this dress when I bought it. It's classy, with just the right amount of sex appeal, but after that night with Cian, I couldn't bring myself to wear it again.

I run my hands over the silky finish. My mind fills with memories of the last time I wore this exact dress. It seems almost fitting to wear it for him again tonight. It's like we are finally getting our second chance — a first date do-over. *This time, the only place I'm running to will be into his arms.*

Cassie helps me finish up my look. She curls my long brown hair into soft waves then applies a thin layer of makeup to my face, giving me a natural look. Once she's finished, I look in the floor-length mirror. Wow! I haven't looked this good in years.

I'm ashamed to say, ever since Croí was born, I've let myself go a little. The only time I ever wear makeup is for work, where I'm always required to look like a walking Mac make-up advertisement. It's nice to look in the mirror and see the old me again. She's been in hiding for so long, and thanks to Cian, she's coming back. Ella the girl, not Ella the mom.

The knock on the front door pulls me back to the present. *He's here.* I head down the hall and open the door for him. My breath catches when I take in the sight before me. I thought Cian Mulligan looked good in a t-shirt and jeans but in a suit. *Holy shit!* The man is pure sex on legs. His normal, messy black hair's tamed slightly. His chiselled face holds just the right amount of stubble. His suit is tailored to perfection, accentuating his broad shoulders and slim waist. *I want to rip it right off him. Down, girl!*

In his hands is the most beautiful bouquet of

sunflowers. *I don't know how he knew, but they're my favourites.* He steps in through the doorway and places a gentle kiss on my cheek. "You look beautiful, Angel."

He places the flowers on the side table, then pulls me into his arms. An uncontrollable shiver travels up my spine when his deep brogue whispers against my neck.

"The last time I saw you in that dress I tore it off with my teeth. Are you hoping for the same result tonight?" *Yes. Well, minus the unplanned pregnancy, but all the rest… hell-to-the-yes!*

An involuntarily moan escapes my lips, making Cian chuckle. His eyes find mine, those stormy blue irises are extra bright tonight, sparking with a look I've only seen him give to Croí. They're filled with love. There is something else there too. Lust. Raw, uncontainable lust.

"You scrub up well yourself," I reply.

He flashes me his knee-weakening dimples, accompanied by a cheeky wink. "I'm just going to say goodnight to our boy then we can head out. Wait right here." He rushes down the hallway, leaving me standing there hornier than a bitch in heat.

That's when I see it, parked at the end of my driveway is a gorgeous black stretch limo. *Oh my God!*

"Are you ready to go?" Cian steps in behind me. *That was quick.* I nod my head *yes. A freaking limo. He got me limo.*

We drive for a few minutes before we pull up to one of L.A.'s top restaurants, *Blu*.

I've only heard of this in Cassie's Gossip magazines. The place has five Michelin stars. The only stars I'm used to is Four Star pizza.

Sometimes it's easy to forget that Cian is famous, but when we step out of the limo, the cameras flashing at us remind me exactly who I am out on a date with. I hear the shouts from the paparazzi, the lights from their cameras blinding me.

Cian, who's the girl?

Cian, does this mean you're off the market?

Cian, is she the one?

Cian, over here.

Cian curses under his breath. He wraps his arms tighter around my waist, whispering quietly in my ear. "Keep your head down and stay close. You'll be fine. If you keep your head down, they won't be able to take a picture of you." I can't help it, my insecurities rise. *Does he not want to be seen with me? Is he ashamed? I'm not some rising star or supermodel.* I push those thoughts to the back of my head. He's only trying to keep me safe from the media shitstorm. Stop over-reacting.

Finally, we push our way into the restaurant, where a blonde woman rushes to greet us. Her eyes roam over Cian in a come-hither kind of way. *Back of bitch, he's mine.*

"Welcome, Mr. Mulligan," she greets him, running her overly long manicured nails over his bicep. He shakes her off, which pleases me to no end. I fight the urge to stick my tongue out at her and shout: *Na, na, na na, nah.* "We have your table ready as requested. Please follow me." She leads us past all the other patrons to a glass elevator. My eyes roam around the expensive restaurant in awe. I've been living like a peasant for years, so this is so surreal. We step inside and she presses the button with the letter R.

The elevator stops, and the doors open onto a rooftop overlooking the whole of Hollywood. My eyes expand to double their original size. *Wow.*

In the centre sits one table set for two. Twinkling fairy lights are strung overhead, and candles dot the rooftop, flicking in the warm breeze, giving off a romantic setting. They've placed vases upon vases of sunflowers all around me. It's beautiful! I feel like I've just stepped into a movie scene. How did he manage all this? Music plays softly in the background. It's magical and romantic.

I turn to look at Cian and he's staring straight at me. "Is this okay?" he asks, pulling at the collar of his shirt.

I push up on my toes and give him a small kiss. "It's amazing, Cian. Thank you."

"Anything to keep that smile on your gorgeous face."

He walks me to our seats, pulling out my chair for me, like a true gentleman. A waiter appears out of nowhere. He takes our order before he is gone again, vanishing into thin air. *Perks of being famous, I guess.*

After our meal, I walk towards the edge of the building, taking in the beautiful city below me. The view from up here is amazing, breath-taking. I feel Cian step behind me. He wraps his arms around my waist and rests his head on my shoulder. Together we look out at the city.

"Come, dance with me?" he requests.

I turn to face him. In his hand is a small remote. He presses a button, and the music starts to flow through the night air. He places the remote on the table and pulls me into his arms. He spins me around and we settle into an easy sway. I rest my head against his chest as he sings the lyrics of Elvis Presley's *I can't help falling in love with you*; with that amazing raspy voice of his. I melt into him, letting him lead me around the rooftop. He spins me out, twirling me under his arm, before pulling me against him again. The lyrics force all the air out of my lungs. Maybe because I can't help falling in love with Cian Mulligan. The song ends but we keep swaying under the light of a thousand stars, and for once, I allow myself to see a happy future — one that belongs to him.

Chapter Seventeen

I Won't Give Up by Jason Mraz

Cian

We stay dancing on the rooftop for what feels like hours. Ella, in my arms, has quickly become one of my favourite pastimes. Her head rests against my shoulder as we sway to, *I won't give up,* by Jason Mraz. If I had to express how I feel about mine and Ella's situation — this song says it all. I will never give up on them. No matter what life may throw at us, I'll make sure we win out in the end. I pull her closer as I lead her around the large rooftop.

I know it seems like I'm rushing into this headfirst, but she is the mother of my child; our circumstances are not normal. We did things a little backward, but I know in the pit of my stomach that she is my endgame.

I'm ready to jump, all in. I'm ready to start our life together as a unit, a team, a family.

I never thought I'd get a second chance with the girl who got away, but now I have her precious body between my arms, there is nothing in the world that will make me let her go.

I catch our waiter from earlier, in the corner of my eye, standing next to the opened elevator. He holds the door with one hand while signalling me that our driver has arrived with the other. *Looks like it's time for my next surprise.*

"Okay, darling, time to go," I whisper into Ella's hair. I place a hand on the small of her back, leading her over to the elevator.

The door closes behind us. I place a small kiss on her forehead before pulling her closer. "Why the sad face, Angel?" I ask, tilting her face towards mine.

"Not sad, just disappointed. I was having fun. Where are we going now?" she asks, her eyebrows raised in curiosity.

I lean closer, whispering in her ear. "You'll have to just wait and see. It's a surprise."

"Surprise, huh? What if I said I don't like surprises?" she teases, her face lit up with that blinding smile of hers.

"What if *I* said you will love *this* surprise?" I throwback with a smile of my own.

"We'll see, Irish."

We make our way through the busy restaurant and out to the limo waiting to bring us to our next destination. There are cameras flashing from all directions. Ella grips my hand tighter; her shoulders straighten with confidence and she lifts her head high, standing proud by my side.

"Are you sure you want to do this? They can be vultures," I ask, keeping my voice low for her ears only.

Her eyes find mine with a look that could bring me to my knees. It bleeds love and determination.

"We're a team, remember? Me, you, and Croí... against the world," she whispers to my ears only.

"Against the world," I repeat.

|***|

About thirty minutes later, our limo pulls up at Atlantic Terminal in Burbank. We step out of the limo onto the small airfield, and immediately, we're greeted by Dave, our personal pilot, who flies us all around the world, usually in our private jet, but tonight he is giving Ella and me a guided tour of the beautiful City of Los Angeles.

"Cian, good to see you. It has been a minute," he greets.

"You too, Dave. How's the family?" I ask.

"They're great, getting bigger every second." He holds his hand out in Ella's direction. "You must be Ella. Nice to meet you. I'm Dave, I'll be your pilot tonight."

Ella's eyes widen with surprise. "Hi, nice to meet you."

Ella's eyes bounce between us and the large helicopter stationed behind him.

"Are we... are we going in that?" She screams with delight. I can hear the happiness sprinkled in her voice. She looks just like a kid on Christmas morning. My chest fills with pride. I did that: I put that glorious smile on her face.

"Oh my God, I've always wanted to do a helicopter ride. This is amazing, wait until I tell Cassie... I'm going on a helicopter," she sings.

Dave and I throw our heads back in laughter. Her excitement is contagious. I watch her closely as she spins around the tarmac in circles — just like Lady Gaga in that new movie. The excitement shining in her hazel eyes is adorable. I vow, there and then, to make her smile like that every fucking day for the rest of my life.

"Okay, kids, let's load up and get this show on the road," Dave suggests.

I help Ella climb up the steps into the helicopter, strapping her securely into the seat. I laugh at the way she is still bouncing up and down. She's fighting to contain her excitement, which I find pretty cute. "This is amazing, I can't believe you booked us a helicopter ride. This is the best first date ever," she claims, making me feel like the king of the world.

I show her how to fit her headset so we can talk while in the air, and she kisses me sweetly once I fit it in place.

The unique rhythmic sound of the blades turning signals our take off. The helicopter lifts off the ground in one swift motion, smooth like an elevator rising. The open cabin allows us a 180-degree view of the city below.

"Are you okay?" I ask as we rise to the sky.

"I'm amazed, thank you, Cian," she replies with delight.

Once we fully ascend, Ella's enthusiasm calms a bit. Her eyes stay focused on the glass, taking in the sites below. I don't think she has even blinked in fear that she might miss something. *God, she is gorgeous.* I make a mental note to thank Rosie. The helicopter was her idea, and it seems Ella really loves it. She is radiant when she's happy, and if her face is anything to go by, she's having a great time.

We fly over Pacific Palisades, Marina Del Rey, and Venice Beach. The view of the beaches is breath-taking. There is nothing like seeing the city from the air. It's amazing.

Ella reaches across and grabs my hand, squeezing it tight. "Thank you so much, Cian. This is so beautiful."

"So are you, Angel." I lift our joined hands, placing little kisses across her knuckles.

I open a bottle of wine I take from the mini cooler box, pouring us both a glass. I pull her close, tucking her in under my arm and together we look out at all the famous sites Los Angeles has to offer. Walt Disney Concert Hall, Dodger Stadium, Beverly Hills, Bel Air, and the Hollywood sign. We don't exchange any words; we just sit together basking in the comfortable silence.

The tour ends when we land on top of the Four Seasons. I booked the Presidential suite for us tonight. I'm not pressuring her into anything, but I need her in my arms. Hopefully, she feels the same. I texted Cassie earlier, asking her if she minds if I kept Ella out for the night. She was more than happy to watch the little guy, giving us some much-needed alone time. I owe her big time.

Ella

Tonight, was beyond magical. There are no other words I can use to describe it. Cian really outdid himself; every detail was perfect. I walk around the presidential suite of The Four Seasons Hotel. *I kid you not, this place is bigger than my freaking house.*

The room has a distinct Cali vibe — bright, modern, and chic. I take in the ceiling to floor-length windows. They give an amazing view of Hollywood Hills and Downtown L.A. Next, I make my way into the bathroom. *Holy mother of marble. Is that a rain-shower? Have I died and gone to bathroom heaven?*

"There you are." Cian's voice comes from behind me. He wraps those tattooed arms around me, pulling me in tight to his chest — my back to his front. I melt into him, resting my head against his collarbone. "This place is gorgeous. I've never seen anything like it in my life. Thank you for bringing me here, and for tonight. It's been amazing."

"No problem at all, Angel. One day soon, I'll show you the world," he states, before peppering my neck with tiny kisses. Goosebumps erupt all over my skin. "Cian," I moan.

"Say it, sweetheart," he replies, his lips barely leaving my skin.

"I need..."

"What Ella? What do you need?"

"You... I need you."

He spins me around to face him, lifting me up so I can wrap my legs around his waist. His hands grip my ass as he takes careful but determined steps towards the bedroom, before dropping me down against the satin sheets covering the California king bed.

"Do you know how long I've waited to have you like this again?" he growls. "Stand up for me," he commands.

I quickly submit to his demand. My skin is on fire, craving his touch. His hands reach for the hem of my dress, and ever so slowly he begins to raise it up over my thighs. His fingers leave a trail of goosebumps along my golden skin. Once he has the dress up and over my head, he takes a step back, admiring my matching black lace bra and panties.

"So beautiful," he states, and with the way his eyes are blazing with desire, I can't help but believe him.

It feels like minutes pass before he kneels before me. Taking a hold of my panties, he pulls, ripping the material in two. *Well, fuck me. That's hot!*

"Lay back for me, sweetheart." His voice is soft yet commanding.

Once I'm where he wants me, he lifts my right leg, kissing his way up from my ankle to my promise land, he stops, just before reaching my centre, taunting me, teasing me. "Please, Cian," I cry out, the need for release stronger than I can bear.

"Patience, Angel," he says, raising my left leg and repeating the same process as before. Only this time, when he reaches my core, he places a delicate kiss right in the crease, where my thigh meets my centre, causing my body to jerk with anticipation.

"Stop teasing," I beg.

"Say please." I can hear the smugness behind those words, and if I wasn't so worked up, I'd probably tell him to fuck off, and he knows that. *Sexual blackmail at its finest.*

"Please, Cian."

His tongue flickers across my clit, each stroke is like a match to gasoline. My body is burning with the fire of the flames. I grab hold of the silk bed sheets, my back arching as he sucks on my clit. He applies just the right amount of pressure to send me spinning into release; one last brush of his tongue makes me erupt, leaving my limbs shaking with the aftershock of my orgasm.

My turn.

Chapter Eighteen

Dance for You by Beyoncé

Ella

I rid Cian of his suit in record time, leaving him standing before me in nothing but a pair of tight black Armani boxers. I roam my hands over his impressive torso, tracing the tattoos that cover his skin. I take in the details of each design; everything from roses to song lyrics cover his arms and shoulders. Knowing Cian — each piece tells its own story. When my eyes land on his chest, I'm transfixed by the silver barbells that adorn his nipples. *Oh, the Lord Jesus, they weren't there before!*

That's when I see it, the tattoo marking the skin of his left pec — right over his heart. A small lock and key, identical to the one that bound us together all those years ago. I run my fingers over the intricate design, allowing my fingertips to follow each curve and line. It's beautiful. *I haven't seen this man naked in six years. When did he get it?* The ink has faded, letting me know that he had it done a few years ago.

"When?" The question comes out barely above a whisper. This tattoo is a clear indication that he never forgot. He has been carrying a piece of me, a piece of us, with him. Every day. He lifts his hand to cover mine, right where it rests over the tattoo on his chest. I can feel his beating heart pounding against my palm.

"I got it just after that first tour with *Sinners*. I couldn't get you out of my head. I knew even back then that my heart belongs to you; I needed to have a piece of you with me, and this — " he presses my hand down against the ink. " — was the only thing I could think of."

Without warning, he leans forward, locking his lips to mine, leaving me utterly breathless.

I kiss my way down his body, starting with the curve of his neck. I take my time savouring the salty taste of his skin. I lick my way down across his collarbone to the tattoo. I run the tip of my tongue across the black lines, causing Cian's body to jerk in response to the sensual touch. "Jesus, El, you're killing me here. I need you now," he moans.

A soft chuckle leaves me. I love this; I love how I can make a man like Cian Mulligan feel helpless and out of control with desire. I gently push him back towards the bed.

"Sit," I command.

I see the heat that burns in his eyes, but he complies. "El, what are you doing, baby?" His voice is filled with need.

I lean down, my mouth hovering over his lips. I hold his gaze with mine. "I know you said you didn't like me dancing for others, but how would you feel about me dancing just for you?"

His eyes close briefly, and his Adam's Apple gulps. When he opens those stormy eyes, they are wilder than I've ever seen.

"What do you say, Irish? Would you like me to dance for you?"

"Yes." That's it, one word.

I leave him sitting on the edge of the bed. I walk confidently over to the iPod dock on the hotel table. I scroll through the selections, coming to a stop when my eyes land on the perfect song for my little tease. Beyoncé's *Dance for You.*

Perfect.

I press play, and the sound of heavy rainfall flows through the surround sound. The clicking of Beyoncé's footsteps matches my own. I strut back towards Cian as the vibration of the synthesizer's echoes around us.

I drag over the nearby desk chair, placing it in Cian's direct line of vision. I take a seat — my back to his front — so he has a clear view of my spine. I fluff my hair, allowing my chestnut waves to cascade down my back

Beyoncé's voice delivers the first line of the song just as I begin to slowly drag my fingers up over the dip of my curves. I glance over my right shoulder to find Cian completely transfixed, his eyes taking in every single sensual movement.

The steady beat of the drum drops. I stand, kicking away the chair from beneath me. Cian's eyes are ablaze with lust, roaming over my body, hypnotized by my every sway.

Just when I think he can't take it anymore, I move to straddle his hips, rocking mine in time to the music. Cian's hands move to cup my ass, pulling me down so he can grind his length against my core. Nothing between us but the thin material of his boxer shorts.

"Fuck me, Ella, I have never been so turned on in my life. I need to get inside you. Now!" The rough, sexy tone to his voice is laced with promise, a promise of what's yet to come.

He frantically removes his black boxer briefs while reaching for protection. He rolls the condom down his impressive length in record time. Next thing I know, he flips me onto my back, his chiselled body towering over mine. His hard cock brushes against my entrance, enticing a moan to escape my lips.

"Say it, Ella."

"I need you."

"Where?" he grumbles.

"Inside me... now!"

I stare up into his midnight blue eyes, as the tip of his cock enters my core. My eyes close at the small sting. It's been six years since I've had a man inside me. Six years since him.

My body clamps around him as he enters me inch by inch. Once he is fully inside me, he takes hold of my cheek. "Open up those beautiful eyes. I want to see you," he states.

I quickly obey. At first, he moves in slow torturous strokes, then he picks up the pace, pounding into me harder and faster to the beat of the song. With each snap of his hips, my body aches with need and desire. My breasts bouncing with every single thrust.

My orgasm is working its way to release when suddenly, he pulls out completely, flipping my body over. He pulls me up onto my knees, plunging back into me, reaching deeper than before, leaving me aching, craving for the delicious high that comes with an earth-shattering orgasm.

He grips my right hip with one hand; he delivers powerful thrust after powerful thrust. With his free hand, he reaches around my body, his fingers pinch my clit with just the right amount of pressure — sending me into the most intense climax of my life.

I grab hold of the headboard to keep myself from collapsing as he pounds into me over and over again before surrendering to his own release. We collapse on the bed, our limbs tangled together. Cian pulls me into his chest, my back to his front. "Please come home with me, Ella?" he asks softly into my ear. I don't know if it's from the afterglow of the best sex of my life, but I reply, "Okay, I'll go home with you."

|***|

The morning sun shines through the large floor to ceiling windows lighting up our hotel room. Last night with Cian was amazing.

I take a minute to bask in the feeling of his arms wrapped protectively around me. His heavy breath against my skin signals that he is still fast asleep. If I could, I would live in this moment forever. My phone buzzes on the locker beside the bed.

It could be Cassie. I reach for it trying not to wake Cian. I unlock it and sure enough, it's her.

1 new message: Cassie

Cassie: Have you seen today's cover of Rockstar Weekly?

Ella: Nope, I'm only awake. Why?

Cassie: Oh, really. (fire emoji) How was it? Is it as big as you remember? (Eggplant emoji)

Ella: Cas!!! You CANNOT ask that.

Cassie: Oh, but I just did...

Ella: What's so important about Rockstar Weekly that you had to wake me up?

Cassie: Oh, shit, sorry. I got DICK-stracted! Lol! Hold on I'll forward you the link now.

Cassie: [[TAP TO DOWNLOAD ATTACHMENT]]

Ella: Omfg! WTF! I'm on the cover of Rockstar Weekly. WHAT THE HELL AM I GOING TO DO?

Cassie: Well, first, STOP SHOUTING AT ME! Secondly, wake up Mr. Orgasmic and get back here. The paparazzi are on the lawn.

Ella: What? Where is Croí?

Cassie: He's fine, I closed the blinds. Just hurry back before it gets any worse.

Ella: Okay, stay inside. I'm coming now.

Cassie: That's what she said. (Eggplant and water droplet emoji)

|***|

After waking Cian, we head straight back to the house. Cassie was right, the place is crawling with paparazzi. *How does Cian put up with this? Is this going to be my life now!*

Eventually, we get inside the house without being mobbed. I'm so far out of my depth here, I don't know what to do. I pace around the living room, running my hands through my hair.

"Ella, you need to calm down," Cian says,

rubbing his hand up and down my back.

"How can I calm down? We can't even leave the house. I'm not famous Cian; I'm not used to my private life been so freaking public," I shout. I feel like I'm suffocating; it's as if someone is squeezing all the air from my lungs. *I knew this was coming. I thought I was prepared — clearly not. I'm going to pass out. There are photographers on my freaking lawn.*

Cian steadies me by gripping my forearms. "Breathe, Ella," he states. "Do you trust me?" he asks

"Yes, completely." I don't hesitate to reply; which shocks me. If you had asked me a few weeks ago, I would've said no.

But, after spending time with Cian, watching him with our son and with the way he treats me — I know his intentions are good. He keeps telling me he is all in; maybe it's time I am too. I'm ready to face whatever storm life gives us because I know Cian will be *my calm* through it all. I focus on my breathing. I can do this. We can do this. We're a team, a family.

"Okay, I'm okay," I offer. I don't know who I'm trying to convince more — him or me.

"Good, now, I want you to pack a bag for yourself and Croí. You're coming back home with me. I'll call Dave, tell him to get the plane ready." He takes hold of my face, locking his eyes to mine. "Just pack the essentials; we can get anything else you need when we land. The Paparazzi won't bother us there, and we can allow everything here to die down." He looks across the room at Cassie.

"You are more than welcome to join us; there is plenty of room in my house. It's going to be crazy here."

Cassie immediately responds, jumping up and down clapping her hands like a deranged seal. "Free holiday, hell yes I'm coming. Let me get my camera and I'm all set," she squeals, running out of the room towards her bedroom.

I take a deep breath, I guess we're going to meet the family.

Ireland here we come!

Chapter Nineteen

Cian

*I*reland — I might be biased, but to me, it is the greatest place on earth. It is a country where beauty, serenity, laughter, and music come together. It's a land full of myths and legends. The one place I've ever felt a true sense of calm and peace. There is just something about our little emerald isle that is indescribably unique. It draws you in, warms your heart, and feeds your soul. I've travelled all around the world, but my internal sat-nav always steers me back to where I belong, Dublin. *Home.*

I'm excited to show Ella my hometown. I'm also nervous; I want her to love it just as much as I do. I want her to be able to see her life here, the future, our future.

I watch Ella as she peers out of the small window beside her seat. The Irish coast comes into view. In the distance, forty shades of green colour the small island.

It will be a big change from the city life of Los Angeles she is used to.

"It's so beautiful," she observes, which puts a large smile on my face.

"Just like you," I reply. I place a small kiss on her forehead and take her hand in mine as we begin our descent down onto the runway of Dublin Airport. I peer over at Cassie and Croí; they're peacefully sleeping. Croí's head rests against Cassie's arm. I guess I better wake them up.

We land without any problems, and after thanking Dave, we collect our luggage and head for arrivals.

Croí slept for most of the journey, but he's still tired, fighting to keep his sleepy eyes open as we make our way through the busy airport. I pick him up so he can rest his head on my shoulder, while Cassie and Ella take care of the bags. At least we don't have far to travel from the airport, fifteen minutes max. My house sits just outside Dublin City in the countryside of North County Dublin. It's not too far from the small village of Oldtown. I'm sure everyone is looking forward to a relaxing evening.

I'm a little nervous to show Ella where I live; it's a big change from the busy City of Los Angeles. There is nothing but green fields surrounding my property. It gives plenty of privacy for someone of my status. The locals here are so used to me by now; they respect my privacy.

I grew up around these parts. Everyone here knows me as the Mulligan boy — not the famous musician. Mostly, I can live a normal enough life. The paparazzi are not as crazy as they are in

America, and thankfully, there are none here today. It's just what Ella and Croí need after that shitshow they witnessed in L.A.

I rang Lily ahead of time. I asked her to pick up a few bits for the house. She had it stocked with a few groceries and prepared a room each for Cassie and Croí. She also took the liberty and went to *Smyths toy store* to kit out a playroom for Croí too. I want my son to feel at home because that's exactly where he is. *Home.* Lily is Cillian's sister, but she also works for the band, catering to all our needs. She is the best at her job. If any of us ever need anything, you can guarantee Lily O'Shea will get it done. She is a take-no-prisoners type of girl. That's why she finds it a walk in the park to babysit our four asses for a living.

We find Rosie waiting for us as we enter Terminal 2. She has been so excited to finally meet her little nephew. She just about broke my eardrum when I called with the news, we were flying home. She insisted on picking us up. I hope she will get along with Ella and Cassie. I love my sister; she's one of my best friends. □

"Hello, handsome. How are you?" she greets Croí, holding her arms wide for a hug. They've spent a lot of time talking — on FaceTime — over the last few weeks.

Croí was also excited to finally meet '*the girl from the phone*'.

He jumps from my arms and runs in her direction. His tiredness is long forgotten.

"Aunt Rosie," he shouts, leaping right into her arms. My chest tightens at the sight.

I watch from a distance as they engulf each other in a bear hug. I wrap my arm around Ella's shoulder, tucking her in tight to my chest.

"I've been replaced," Cassie slucks, holding her hand to her chest.

"Awh, Cas, don't worry he still loves you," Ella offers through her laughter.

"I know, I just don't want to share him. He has been just mine for so long," she states, looking a little like a spoiled child who isn't getting her way. I swear she is seconds away from stamping her foot.

"Come, Aunt Rosie, come meet my mom and Aunt Cassie," Croí grabs Rosie's hand, pulling her in our direction.

Ella stiffens under my arm. Leaning down, I whisper in her ear. "Don't worry, she will love you."

Her hazel eyes meet mine, and I want to add four more words to that statement. *Just like I do.*

|***|

When we arrive back at the house, we're greeted by the whole gang. Mam, Dad, Cillian, Ciaran, Conor, Lily, and Cillian's Mam, Mary. I introduce everyone and watch silently, leaning up against the doorway as everyone fawns all over Ella and Cassie. Croí has yet to let go of my leg; he has been hiding behind me since we arrived. It must be very overwhelming for him to meet all these people.

They aren't exactly quiet.

"Hello, darling. It's so good to finally meet you. My name is Maggie, but you can call me Ma," my mam greets Ella, pulling her into a warm motherly hug. Ella seems a little awkward at first, but suddenly she seems to relax, her arms wrapping around my mam's petite frame.

When they finally pull apart, Croí peeks out from behind my leg. His eyes are wide as he scans all the new faces.

"And who do we have here?" my mam asks. She slowly approaches us, kneeling to Croí's level. "Hi, sweetheart. I'm your Granny Mag," she offers him with a wide smile.

He looks up at me, silently asking me if it's okay to approach her. I nod my head in encouragement. I gently place my hand on his shoulder, letting him know I'm right behind him.

He takes two very careful steps towards her. "Hi... I'm Croí."

"Nice to meet you. Would it be okay if I gave you a hug?" she questions. She tries hard to hide the tears welling in her eyes. When Croí steps into her open arms, she pulls him in, squeezing him tight. Her eyes meet mine over Croí's shoulder, and I see the small tear escape down her cheek. She mouths her next words to me. "He is so beautiful."

After a moment, Mam stands, wiping her cheek with her hand. "Okay, who's for tea?" she asks, sniffing back her emotions. She will be an amazing Granny. That woman has more love to give than anyone I've ever met.

I introduce them to everyone else. Hopefully, they all feel welcomed. We spend the next hour sitting around while everyone gets to know Ella, Croí and Cassie. Croí dozes off in my lap, so I show Ella to the room Lily had set up for him.

I gently place him into bed, kissing his cheek. "Goodnight buddy."

"Goodnight Dad."

"Will you be okay here?" I say to Ella as she scans the new books Lily bought for Croí. She turns to face me. "Yes, I'll be fine, go catch up with everyone. I'll be right down," she pushes up onto her toes, placing a small kiss against my lips.

"You're sure?"

"Positive. Go." She smiles. I kiss her once more before heading down the stairs to find Lily. I need to find out what she found in those records I asked her to dig up. Time to find out who the fuck kept my kid from me for six years.

|***|

I find Lily in the kitchen. She sits at the table, her head stuck in her laptop. Her fingers move across the keys at lightning speed.

"Hey Lil," I say, taking the seat beside her.

"Hey, I got that stuff for you." She looks around the room for prying eyes, and when she realizes we're alone, she pulls a large brown folder from her bag. She taps the top with her long nails. "It's all in here, but I have to warn you Cian, you won't like what you'll see."

I flip open the folder where I find every single correspondence Ella ever sent to Sham-Rock Records regarding her and Croí. I read over every word and my anger builds. He knew. He knew all about my son, and yet he never told me.

I stand from the chair with force, causing it to fall over. "Thanks, Lily," I grumble.

"Cian, maybe you should take a minute to calm yourself down," she suggests.

I don't reply; instead, I storm out of the room, seeking the man that stole precious time I can never get back.

"Dad, a word, please?" I force out, desperately trying to keep my voice calm when on the inside I'm ready to tear down this house.

"Yes, sure." He looks nervous and so he should.

I walk down the long hallway to my office, the sound of his footsteps clicking behind me. I open the door and make my way inside. I perch myself on the edge of my oak desk, crossing my arms over my chest. He hesitates in the doorway before finally stepping inside. I motion for him to close the door behind him.

"What's this about, son?" he asks in his usual controlling tone. What my Mam sees in him, I'll never know.

"Don't give me that. You knew, didn't you? For six fucking years... you knew I had a son, and you kept that piece of information from me. Now I want to know why," I scold, the rage burning under my skin like a bonfire.

He pulls at his shirt collar; I've never in my life raised my voice at him. Once upon a time, the man standing before me was my hero, was being the important word. I don't understand why he would feel the need to hide something so crucial from me.

A few days ago, when I had contacted Lily, asking her to dig into the band's emails and call lists to find anything related to Ella, I wasn't expecting to find it was my father. My own fucking flesh and blood. Daddy dearest kept silent about that information. Probably because he knew deep down, I would have dropped everything to be with my family and he would be out of pocket.

As part owner of Sham-Rock Records, Dad has been making a serious amount of cash of the back of 4Clover for years. God forbid that money train ran dry. Just imagine if the lead singer was to pack his shit to care for his son. My God, I'm so fucking angry with him. How could he do something so cold-hearted?

"Son, please just hear me out. I thought it was for the best. The band had just hit it big. You didn't need the distraction."

"Do NOT call me son. You lost that right when you kept MY SON hidden from me for six fucking years, and I didn't need the distraction... What the fuck is wrong with you? Croí is my child, not some toy. I had a right to know. It was NOT your choice to make; it was mine... and you kept it from me.

How dare you try to defend your actions?"

"I thought I was protecting you, Cian. You didn't know this girl from Adam. She could have been a crazy fan, for all I knew the kid might not have even been yours."

"Bullshit! Ella told me she sent pictures; she told me she offered DNA testing, but you refused to even listen to a word she had to say, and because of that, I missed out on my son growing up. I missed his first tooth, his first steps. I missed him riding a bike for the first time. I missed his first day at kindergarten. I missed his first fucking word. All because you're a selfish son of a bitch.

So, unless you can give me a goddamn good reason why you felt the need to keep them both from me, I suggest you get your shit and get the fuck out of my house." I've never wanted to hit someone so much in my entire life. Just the sight of the man I once idolized is making me sick.

"Cian, I'm sorry, okay? If I could take it back, I would. Seeing you with Croí tonight, seeing how good you are with him — it reminded me a lot of you and me all those years ago. I'm sorry I didn't tell you about him. You're right, you deserved to know."

That's my dad for you, a master manipulator. He is king at turning situations around to make you feel like the bad guy. He's trying to guilt me; it's how he's made it so far in the cutthroat world that is the music industry.

I don't care what he has to say though; he crossed

a line with me when he kept that information from me. I had enough of his games. I'm done, and if I have anything to do with it, his career will be too.

"Get the hell out of my house. You are not welcome here."

"Son, please."

"I said, get the fuck out."

He turns on his heel and heads for the door. Good fucking riddance to bad rubbish.

A few minutes later, Rosie appears in the doorway. "Hey, brother, you okay?"

I lift my head up from where it's resting in my palms. "Honestly, no. How could he do this to me? They needed me, Ro, and I wasn't there, all so he could keep lining his pockets. Who does that?" I shove my hands through my hair in frustration.

"I know all about Dad and his games, Cian, trust me on that. He will do anything for money, even use his own children as pawns in his sick little games," she claims, her head hung low.

"Sean?" I question. She nods her head yes.

I fucking knew there was something fishy about Rosie and Sean's relationship. It shouldn't surprise me that Dad is the one behind it.

"Will you go ahead with the wedding?" I ask.

"Honestly, Cian, I don't know."

We speak a little more about her situation and decide that something must be done to stop this power trip my dad is on. The only question is how?

Chapter Twenty

Home by Phillip Phillips

Cian

I spend the next half an hour going through a few scenarios with Rosie. Eventually, we decide to put everything Dad related on hold — at least until she figures out what to do about her upcoming nuptials.

"Thanks for that, Cian. It's been good getting everything off my chest." She wraps her arms around me in a sisterly hug.

"Anytime, Ringa Rosie," I comfort her. She might be a pain in my ass, but she's my sister, and I would do anything to protect her and make her happy.

Together, we make our way to the kitchen. I find Ella perched on one of the high bar stools around the island. Her head is thrown back in laughter as she chats excitedly with Cassie and Lily.

Looking at them all together, you would swear they've known each other their whole lives. Honestly, it's a bit surprising. Lily doesn't take to people easily. She has a very small circle that she guards like a little Pitbull. So, I'm glad she's enjoying Ella and Cassie's company. She is a big part of my life too; she is basically family.

I'm still a little unsure about whether to tell Ella about my conversation with my dad or not. I want to be one hundred percent with her, but I don't want to drag up the past either. She hasn't stopped smiling since we arrived, and I know finding out my dad of all people was the one thing standing in the way of me being a part of their lives would crush her. I hate this; I hate that he put me in this position. I feel like we just got to a happy place; I don't want to have to pull the rug from under us.

"Hello, handsome," Ella greets when she spots me leaning in the doorway against the door frame with my arms folded across my chest.

I hide away any thoughts relating to my dad and push off the doorway to move towards her. "Hey, you." I lean forward and place a kiss on her forehead. "How are you holding up? I hope Lily here isn't filling your beautiful head with stories." I wink.

I move to stand behind her, wrapping my arms around her waist, my head resting on top of hers. She fits nicely under my chin, like my matching puzzle piece.

Lily holds out her hands in a way that screams, *'Don't shoot the messenger!'*.

A small chuckle leaves Ella's mouth. "No, she's just been telling us about the time she paid you ten

Euros to steal Ciaran's shower gel so she could fill it with itching powder." Her voice dances with amusement.

How Ciaran and Lily haven't killed each other over the years is beyond me. They've had this tug of war thing going on since we were kids. Lily usually comes out the winner. They both spend more time trying to one-up each other than actually sorting out the obvious tension between them.

"Oh, what about the time you, Ciaran, and Cillian thought it would be funny to fill all the Oreos with toothpaste, then got so stoned that you forgot you did it, then ate them all yourselves," Rosie joins in. She pops one of Mam's chocolate chip cookies into her mouth then takes the seat beside Cassie.

Cassie is now full out laughing, red wine spraying from her mouth. "Oh my god, I wish I met you all sooner; you sound like my kind of people."

"We've had some good times, also some pretty shitty ones too, but that's a story for another day," Lily states, her face void of any emotion. I don't know how she does it; she is a master at hiding her feelings.

Ella yawns with a loud sigh. It's been a really long day; I'd say her jet lag is starting to kick in.

"Let's head to bed, sweetheart. You sound exhausted," I whisper against her neck.

She tilts her head back so her eyes can meet mine. "Yeah, it just came over me suddenly. Bed sounds amazing right now."

We say a quick goodnight to the girls. I offer

Rosie and Lily the other guest room to stay the night, to save them driving back to their shared house. They decide to stay, so I leave Cassie in their capable hands and take my angel to bed.

We check on Croí on the way, and thankfully, he is fast asleep. I showed him where my room was earlier — just in case he wakes in the middle of the night in a strange house. I don't want him to get disoriented. We also set up a monitor so we can hear if he wakes. It's probably a bit excessive for a six-year-old, but he is in a new environment, and I want to make sure he settles in without a hitch.

We climb into bed, and Ella falls asleep before her head even hits the pillow. I won't say I'm not disappointed because I can't wait to have her again, but if I get my way, we will have plenty of time for that. I pull her close to my chest, wrapping my arms around her tiny frame. I bury my face in her hair and bask in the feeling of her laying in my arms.

"Goodnight, Angel," I whisper, kissing the hair on her head.

Even in her comatose state, she mumbles out a reply. "Night, Irish."

|***|

The next morning, Rosie and Lily take Cassie to Blanchardstown Shopping Centre to pick up a few bits and pieces. May God help her because if those two get loose in Penny's, they could be gone for hours. That shop is like a black hole for women;

once they go in, they might never come out. She'll either love it or she will be sending SOS messages before the day is over.

Since the band has a free morning, I thought some family time would do Ella and Croí some good. It also might help me take my mind off last night's turn of events. I decide to bring Croí and Ella into the Phoenix Park. It's the biggest enclosed park in Europe and the home of Dublin Zoo.

It saddens me to think that they never did anything like this before because of their lack of money. Even more so, because I have enough to last me several lifetimes. Without sounding like a wanker, I'm also happy I get to share these memories with them. It will be one of Croí's first that I get to witness.

I find it so much easier to blend into a crowd in Ireland. If I bundle up, not many people notice who I am, unless they spot the tattoos on my hands. And even at that, not many people approach me. I get asked for the odd picture and a few autographs, but here in Dublin, I'm able to relax and take a break from the madness.

It is a crisp October day. I love days like these; when the sun is shining low in the sky, but there's still a cool bite of cold in the air; the days you've to wrap up in warm clothes. The air holds a freshness that reminds me I'm home, and the autumn leaves cover the ground in a ray of colours from yellow, gold, red, and greens.

Autumn is my favourite season to be here; once

the rain holds off, Ireland is really a spectacularly beautiful place.

Once we get to the park, we agree to take a stroll around the forestry hand in hand before heading to the zoo. With the weather as nice as it is, it would be a shame not to. As we walk, I realize how much I want this. Ella, Croí, and me. Forever. I know it's only been a few weeks, but as soon as I know she is ready, I want to make things more permanent. *Mrs. Ella Mulligan.*

I open the backpack Mom packed us earlier. I pull out some carrots so Croí can feed the deer.

"Did you know? These are Santa's reindeer," I tell him. His eyes widen at the tale my mam told me when I was his age.

"Really?" he questions, his eyes darting between me and Ella for confirmation.

"Yeah, of course. Santa leaves them here to rest every year. Then once it gets nearer to Christmas, he brings them back to the North Pole to get ready for their big trip around the world," I explain.

"Wow, how cool."

Once we finish feeding them all the carrots, we head to the famous Pope's Cross. We climb up the countless steps before rolling back down the large hill behind it. Croí screams his little head off with excitement and insists we do it four more times. Finally, we head to the zoo where we spend three hours walking around looking at all the animals.

Croí is in awe of the Dinosaur exhibition. He spouts off so many facts with ease. He seems to be enjoying himself, and that's all I can ask for. After the dinosaur exhibit, we move to the African Safari, where Croí tells me that the Giraffes are his favourite.

"Dad, did you know that giraffes have seven bones in their necks? It's the same as we do, but ours are much smaller," he says, surprising me with that little fact.

"No, I didn't," I reply with a genuine smile.

"Yep. They're super tall, like a whole seventeen feet, but not like seventeen of my feet cause my feet aren't very big," he states. *God, I love this kid.*

We finally make it around the large zoo, stopping at the gift shop so we can buy Croí his own giraffe teddy. He is exhausted, so I lift him up onto my shoulders as we walk back to the car. The poor little fella has walked the legs off himself today.

"Are you guys hungry?" I ask Ella as we exit the park and head for the motorway.

Ella's hand covers mine on top of the gear stick, her fingers interlocking with mine. I take a quick look at her gorgeous face giving her a large smile before averting my eyes back to the road ahead.

"Yeah, I could eat."

"How does McDonald's sound?" I suggest to them both.

"Like the bestest day ever!" Croí shouts from his new booster seat in the back. Also, courtesy of Lily. I make a mental note to thank her later; the girl thought of everything.

Ella's hand squeezes mine a little tighter.

"Thanks, so much for today, Cian. It really means a lot; we had a great time."

I lift her hand to my lips, placing a small kiss on her knuckles. "You don't have to thank me, El. We're family. Today with you and Croí was one of the best days of my life. I'm so sorry I missed out on the early days with you both. I have a lot of catching up to do. I promised you I'd show you the world someday. This is just the beginning."

A huge smile lights up her face. *Beautiful. Mine.*

"I love you, Ella." The words slip out of my mouth before I can stop them. This was not how I planned on telling her, but it's out there now. She leans across the centre console, kissing my cheek.

"That's good, Irish. Because I love you too," she says, sitting back into her seat with a smile that could light up the world adoring her face.

Maybe Croí was on to something. I think this is the bestest day ever.

Chapter Twenty-One

Black Magic by Little Mix

Ella

I am so in love with Ireland. I don't think I ever want to leave. It's so different from L.A., more relaxed, peaceful even. Cian's family welcomed us with open arms and for the first time — since I lost Nana — I finally feel like I've found somewhere I belong. Somewhere that feels like home.

Cian's house is a beautiful five-bedroom stone bungalow, set in the breath-taking countryside of County Dublin. The house itself has a warm, homey feel, including a large country-style kitchen complete with a range cooker and stove. The backyard is what dreams are made of — the picture of something you would find in a landscape magazine.

Cian keeps it beautifully maintained with an abundance of flowers and shrubs. The two acres of perfectly manicured grass is a rich shade of green, and the large trees that surround the property line give him the privacy he needs.

There is also a built-in BBQ area complete with

its own bar and fire pit for the cooler Irish evenings. I could easily see myself living here. *If I'm being honest, Cian might have to forcefully remove me. It's like heaven on earth.*

I find it extremely hard to believe it's located only twenty minutes from Dublin City Centre. There is nothing but green fields surrounding his property giving you the sense of rural Ireland, but you're still close enough to the buzz of city life. *The best of both worlds.*

I still haven't talked to Cian about what we plan on doing after Rosie's Wedding. It's getting closer, and we haven't once discussed what we will do when it's time for me to go back to L.A.

I know without any doubt if Cian were to ask me to stay here, I would. There is nothing for me back home aside from Nana's house. Maybe we could keep it for when we travel to the States for Cian's band business. I've even contemplated convincing Cassie to stay here too. She's a photographer, so she can work from anywhere. She's family and I don't know how I'd feel about being in a different continent over 5,000 miles away from her.

Cassie decided to do a tour of Dublin city today. She is meeting up with a friend she knows from high school who moved here a few years back. Hopefully, she'll fall in love with this little island and never want to leave.

Cian is tied up with 4Clover business today, and Maggie, Cian's Mom, has offered to take Croí to the National Aquatic Centre for some granny/grandson bonding. She loves that little boy just as much as he loves her. Watching them interact pulls at my heartstrings. Nana and I were so close when she was alive; it's nice to see Croí build the same bond with Cian's mother.

Rosie called earlier, inviting me to spend the day with her and her best friend, Lily. I spent a few hours chatting with them the night we arrived. She should be here any minute to pick me up. I haven't had many girlfriends over the years. I was focused on surviving and providing for Croí. I didn't have time to make friends or socialize. The ladies remind me so much of myself and Cassie, so I'm looking forward to getting to know them. From what I gather, it was Rosie's fiancé's bachelor party in L.A. where Cian found me again. I have met all the 4Clover boys since then, but I've still to meet Sean.

In all my twenty-seven years, I've never met a bride-to-be who is as relaxed as Rosie. She avoids any mention of her big day. You would think she would be more excited by the fact she's getting married. She barely uttered a word — not even the small details like flowers or colour scheme. She is so laid back about the whole thing; it makes me wonder if it's really what she wants.

|***|

We are sitting in Rosie and Lily's gorgeous living room, everything is beautiful, so detailed and meticulously decorated. The room's painted a soft grey, giving it a modern feel. Rosie is an interior designer; she's accentuated the white sofa with cushions and chunky blankets in blush pinks and teal blues, giving just the right contrast between male and female. The centre of the floor is covered with the softest, teal-coloured rug I've ever touched. It reminds me of that scene in *Get Him to the Greek*. *Stroke the furry wall.*

The coffee table is made of mirrored glass, making the overhead chandelier shine a kaleidoscope of colours along the walls. I make a mental note to warn Croí about touching it when he comes here to visit. *His sticky hands would crucify that poor table.* The place is to die for, and I need to suppress the urge to pull out my phone and snap a few pictures for my Pinterest board titled: Living the dream.

Lily is seated on the leather cuddle chair, while Rosie and I are on either side of the matching three-seater. We get cozy, just chatting and getting to know one another a bit better over some wine and snacks. *The best kind of girls' night.*

Rosie is Cian's sister and he's mentioned once or twice that Lily is like a sister to him too, so I want to make a good impression. We're all the same age, which is a plus. After having too many drinks, Rosie asks me all about how Cian and I met the first time. I give them both a detailed description of that Valentine's night at Jars Bar.

They both *oh* and *awe* over the story of how we bumped into each other, *literally.*

"Who knew Cian could be romantic?" Lily says, her eyes wide with shock.

Rosie's next declaration doesn't really shock me. It just confirms what I have already observed about her older brother.

"Cian has always been a bit intense. He leads with his heart and then his head follows. So, if he says he loves you, you can be sure it's wholly and completely. He doesn't do things in half measures; he never did." She tucks her legs beneath her and turns to face me.

"Even when we were kids, he was always the protective one. He was always doing everything he could for the ones he loves. He is extremely driven and passionate; that's why he's become so successful.

He is fuelled by love; his love for music, for the band, for his family, and now his love for you and little Croí. Don't let his intensity scare you. I know my brother like the back of my hand; he will dive into your relationship headfirst.

He has always known exactly what he wants from life and nothing can deter him from achieving it." She gazes at me. Her eyes are filled with the unspoken question. *Do you love my brother?* Thankfully, Lily interrupts before I can answer.

"I agree, I've known Cian for most of my life and he will do everything and anything for the ones closest to him. It's just who he is," Lily says, reaching for the bottle of wine sitting on the glass coffee table.

I know exactly where they're coming from. Cian can be very intense, but when it comes to our relationship, I am just as invested as he is.

All the qualities that should scare me away only make me love him more.

Cian and I decided that we are in this together, as a family, a team.

So, I give them a reassuring smile and try to change the subject to take the focus off me.

"So how did you and Sean get together?" I question Rosie, genuinely curious about their relationship. *They don't even live together.*

Rosie lifts her glass of West Coast Cooler to her lips taking a big gulp before replying, "We met in primary school; that's the equivalent to your elementary school. We never really talked much until our late teens.

We started casually dating at about twenty, nothing serious."

She pauses, taking a deep breath before continuing, "We were on and off more times than my Mam's kettle. Then at about twenty-two, we got a bit more serious." She picks at her pristine nail polish.

She doesn't portray a woman in love — a woman in distress, more like. "He was in College obtaining his Business Masters in Dublin Business School, and I was at the National College of Art and Design getting my degree in Interior Design. We would go out on a few dinner dates and attend business functions together at our parents' request.

Sean's dad is the owner of Morgan & Sons Entertainment Law Firm, which, of course, pleased my dad to no end. Good for business, he would say," Rosie mocks. "So anyway, fast forward a few years and some fairly standard sex later, and here we are." She lifts the glass *again*, this time, draining it to the last drop.

"Jesus, my love garden is mourning for you. That story was about as depressing as a Lana Del Ray album," Lily fake cries into her throw cushion. "Don't get me wrong, I love me some Lana, especially when I need a good cry, but the girl could depress a motivational speaker," she announces, holding her chest to add to her dramatics.

Okay, so Lily has a point; that wasn't the great love story I was expecting to hear, and if it was me, I would be running the other way. I wonder why she's marrying someone that she clearly doesn't love.

"Why marry him then?" *Shit! There goes that filter again.* "I'm sorry, I'm being intrusive. Don't answer that," I blurt. *Damn me and my big mouth.*

Lily tries to hide behind one of the million throw cushions, but it does nothing to hide her muffled laughter.

Rosie throws her own cushion at Lily, hitting her in the boob. Rosie turns back to face me. "It's okay, you're only voicing what you think, and if being friends with *No Filter* over there," she points at Lily, "has taught me anything, it's that honesty is the foundation of the best friendships."

"Hear hear," Lily shouts raising her wine bottle before taking a swig. *Yes, I said bottle, not glass.*

"Enough about me and my soon-to-be husband's microscopic dick.

What you should be asking is why Miss Anti-Commitment over there is still single.

That's a story we are all dying to hear." Rosie laughs, turning my focus to Lily. She shoots Rosie a dagger stare, and I know it's a story I want to hear.

"I am not anti-commitment, more anti-manwhores," Lily protests.

Rosie raises her perfectly arched brows at her friend, daring her to continue.

Lily holds her hands out in surrender. "Okay, maybe I am a little, but that's only because men are all assholes. Let me put it like this: Men are like a pair of tights, they either run, cling too much, or don't fit right in the crotch.

No, thank you. I need a man to be like my coffee. Strong, hot, and keeping me up all night. Unlike some people I know," she points at Rosie with her wine bottle, "I will not settle for less. My Notorious V.A.G. deserves the best!"

"Notorious V.A.G.," I squeal with a laugh. Rosie is doubled over, her giggles making her Rosé squirt out her nose.

"Where do you even pull these names from? First, it was *'Banana Basket'*, then *'The Cock Sock'*. Oh, and let's not forget... *The Death of Adam,"* Rosie coughs out, gasping for breath.

"Oh, I completely forgot about *The Death of Adam*. That one was classic," Lily states with a proud grin.

I raise my brow, staring at them in confusion. *I don't really get that one.*

"Care to explain?" I say.

"You know because of Adam and Eve. You and I both know, it was HER forbidden fruit that killed that poor bastard, not an apple. Therefore," she motions to her lady bits, "*The Death of Adam*," Lily states, shrugging her shoulders.

"Who's Adam?" a masculine voice booms from the hallway. Ciaran's head pops into view through the glass double doors. I haven't spoken to him much over the last few days, but I remember him as the guy in the Guns 'N' Roses T-shirt all those years ago.

He waltzes into the sitting room like he owns the place and plops himself down in the vacant ottoman.

"What are you lovely ladies talking about?" he asks. He kicks off his shoes and lifts his feet to rest on Lily's lap.

I swear I hear Lily growl at him underneath her breath. *Interesting, I wonder if this is who made her swear off the D?*

"What are you doing here? This is a lady only zone, and I'm pretty sure that means no dicks allowed. The last time I checked you were the biggest dick of them all," Lily sasses at Ciaran. With a flick of her hand, she pushes his feet off her lap down to the floor.

"Last time I checked, you didn't seem to mind my big dick, Lilyanna," he throws back. His eyes are like laser beams, fixated on her. The tension between them can cut glass.

Lily matches his glare with one of her own, and her lips curl into a pouty smile. "Yeah well, in the words of Ariana Grande...Thank U, Next!" She waves him off like a bad smell.

"Aw, Lilybug, why do you have to go and hurt his feelings? Everyone knows My *Big Friendly Giant*, is the most sought-after piece of equipment on the market."

Ciaran cups his penis like she hurt its — or as Ciaran said his — feelings. *Why do men always refer to their appendages in the third person?*

"Well, you know what they say, Ciaran: low market prices attract the most customers."

I look at Rosie to gauge her reaction on the pair, but she just mouths, *"You'll get used to it."* I make a mental note to ask Cian about their story later.

"So, Ciaran," Rosie interrupts "If you're here, does that mean my brother is at home?"

"Yeah, I dropped him off on the way here," he answers.

"And, why are you here again?" Lily questions him.

"I came to see my favourite girl." He winks at her.

"Fuck off," Lily says, holding up her middle finger.

"Fuck me," he replies, sticking his index finger through the circle he made with his other hand.

"Okay, well I've had enough of whatever weird roleplay this is... Ella, you ready to go? I think these two need a minute to fuck or kill each other, whatever works," Rosie stands, holding her hands out to help me up from the couch.

"Emm... yeah." I take her hand, and she pulls me up. "Bye, guys."

"Rosie, bring the trash with you," Lily shouts as Ciaran grips her legs pulling her onto the floor.

"Did you just call me trash?" He laughs, attacking her sides with his fingers. She cries out mercy, but he continues his assault.

"Let's go before they get any worse." Rosie rolls her eyes and makes her way to the door with me only a step behind her.

I hear Lily scream out as the door closes behind us. "Take me with you before I chop his dick off and feed it to my Tamagotchi cat."

Chapter Twenty-Two

Cian

I flip open the lid of my bottle, chugging down half of the lime-flavoured water in seconds. Over the past six hours, I've strained my voice from singing non-stop. I move to the large brown leather couch in the corner and flop back onto it.

I lean my head back against the soft leather and close my eyes. *Fuck me, I'm exhausted.* I forgot how tiring recording can be. We are usually so in sync, but today, we just aren't gelling the way we normally do.

My phone vibrates against my leg for what feels like the millionth time. I reach into my pocket to retrieve it. I click the lock button on the side, and I'm greeted with the name of the last person I want to hear from. *Dad.*

I glare at the twelve new messages blinking on the home screen of my iPhone X. They're all unanswered texts from him. He has been rather persistent in his attempts, but I'm not giving in. He went too far. There are no words to describe the anger I feel towards him right now. What father keeps such vital information from his son for six-fucking-years. I shove my phone back into my jeans pocket, blow out a frustrated breath, and head back towards the microphone. I can't deal with his shit right now. I have music to make.

We are currently recording new material for our upcoming album. We have one more track to lay down before I can get home to my family for the night. Even though I am shattered tired and my voice is raw, I don't mind. This next track is mine; it's a song I wrote for Ella. I've been working on it since I found her again. I'm not ready for her to hear it yet, but hopefully, someday soon.

"Okay boys, from the top on three," Mark's voice booms through the overhead intercom system.

Ciaran counts us in with steady four beats against the skins of his drum kit. Cillian follows him by adding his distinct epic riffs. Conor joins, adding just the right amount of bass. I wait for my cue and once the melody reaches its sweet spot, I open my mouth, pouring all the love I feel for Ella into every syllable of every lyric.

I saw you from across the bar,
I didn't know your name.
I knew you were special,
there was something 'bout your face.
I started walking towards you,
to introduce myself.
You crashed right into me.

One moment, and I fell.
When the night was over,
I didn't want to go.
I took your hand in mine
and asked you: "Could I walk you home?"
We walked and talked for hours,
I told you all my dreams.
It was at that moment,
I knew you were meant for me.
Years have separated us,
my feelings never changed.
Lady Luck, she brought you back,
into my arms again.
This time, it is forever,
And I want you to know:
Now you're back in my life,
I'm never letting go.
So baby, can you give me,
this moment I still seek.
I'll promise you forever,
my soul and heart to keep.
I'm asking you this question?
The biggest of my life.
I'm on one knee as I ask thee;
Will you be my wife?

"Sounds great, guys. One more time."

|***|

I'm both mentally and physically drained from today. I am glad I'm finally home. Ciaran dropped me off on his way to Rosie and Lily's, so I'm hoping Ella will be home. I push open the front door and shout, "Anyone home?"

"Dad! You're back." Croí comes barrelling down the long hallway. He runs straight into my open arms, and my chest tightens with emotion. It still hits me now and then — I am a dad. I love coming home to such a welcoming reception; it only solidifies how much I want this. *Them here, with me. Permanently.*

Before I have a chance to even take my coat off, Croí launches into a story about his day at the National Aquatic Centre. "There was this massive slide. We got on these huge yellow double doughnut rings, and we went down the biggest tunnel I've ever seen. It was AMAZING! Then, we ended up stuck in the baby pirate ship pool. Some kid pooped in the lazy river, so the lifeguards had to shut the place down. It was just there, floating around while the staff tried fishing it out with their nets. One lifeguard tried to reach, and he fell right into the water... It was the funniest thing EVER!" *Jesus, kid, take a breath.*

"Cian, honey is that you?" my mam calls from the kitchen.

"Yeah, Ma." I pick Croí up, planting him on top of my shoulders, together we make our way to the kitchen. "Let's go, buddy."

"Is Ella still out?" I ask my Mam upon entering the kitchen.

"Yes, she is still with Rosie. She phoned a few

minutes ago; they're on the way. How was the studio? Did you get all you need to do done?" she asks, never once lifting her gaze from the sink full of dishes.

She dries her soapy hands in the towel before hanging it over her shoulder. She turns to face us. Her gaze locks on me, her eyes flicking between me and my son, who's still perched on my shoulders. I don't need to be a mind reader to know what she is thinking. *Her two boys.* There is nothing but love shining in her eyes, and the smile on her face is gleaming. "Croí, darling, why don't you jump down from there and go wash those hands?" she requests in her loving tone.

"Yes, Nana." He carefully climbs down off my back, then runs out the door to the bathroom under the stairs.

"How was he today?" I question. I stride to the empty stools around the breakfast counter and take a seat.

"He was perfect, we had such a great day. God, Cian, he reminds me so much of you. The resemblance is uncanny. Even his mannerisms are all you. It makes me sad to think about all the years we missed out on." Her hand lands on my arm. She looks at me with saddened eyes.

I'm ninety-nine-point-nine percent certain my mam knew absolutely nothing of my Da's shady dealings. Maggie Mulligan is not the type of woman who sweeps things under the rug. Family is important to her. Through the years, she taught

Rosie and me the importance of being a team, a unit.

The next question ripples from my mouth before I have a chance to stop it. "Did Da tell you?" I know this isn't the best way to approach this conversation, but I need to know.

"Tell me what love?" Her eyebrows crinkle together.

I stare her down, trying to gauge whether she knew. Has she been keeping them from me too?

"Did Dad tell you about Ella, about her contacting him all those years ago? I recently found out he knew all about my son all this time. So, I need to ask, did you know?"

Her blue eyes widen, her face turning a ghostly shade of white. If I had to judge by that reaction, she had no idea. She knew nothing of how cruel her husband could be, how manipulative he has become. The power and money have gone to his head. My heart breaks when I see the tears escape her eyes. They slide down her cheeks like tiny droplets of rain. I engulf her in my arms offering her comfort.

"I'm... I'm so sorry Cian. I had no idea. I would never... please believe me.

I would never keep that precious little boy from you. He is family.

Our blood. Every child deserves to know their parents. How could the man I married do such a horrendous thing?" She sobs into my chest.

It's hard for me to see my mam's usually well-kept appearance fade. This tiny woman has been a pillar of strength all throughout my life. She helped me through the toughest of times with nothing but love and understanding.

After a moment, she pulls out of my hold. She clears her throat and pushes her narrow shoulders back. Her back straightens and she unties the apron from her waist.

She gives me a quick peck on the cheek. "Darling, I will be back. I have a few things I need to handle. If you and Ella don't mind, I'll be sleeping here for a few days. Don't worry about making up a bed; I'll do it when I get back." The strength in her voice is something that only a mother possesses.

"Yeah, Ma, that's fine... I'm sorry about all this. I didn't mean to cause trouble between you and Da."

"You listen to me, Cian Patrick Mulligan. You have absolutely nothing to be sorry for. I love you, and I love that boy. Will I be having words with your father? Yes, I will, and you can expect them to be anything but pleasant. Nobody hurts my babies. Not even the man I married. I am your mother, and I will always be in one of three places: standing in front of you to cheer you on, standing beside you to hold your hand, or standing behind you to watch your back. My babies come first, no matter what."

She pulls me in for one more quick embrace, and then she's gone.

Good luck, Dad. You will need it.

Ella

Rosie and I head back to Cian's house, leaving Lily and Ciaran to their own devices.

I'm still not sure if leaving them together in such close proximity is a good idea, but Rosie assured me they'd be fine.

"What's their story, anyway?" I ask. When I saw the way they reacted with each other, curiosity took over.

"Well, nobody really knows. One minute, they kill each other, the next, well, let's just say Ciaran wasn't joking when he implied that Lily knows exactly how big he is." Rosie pauses for a moment; her eyes hold a look that suggests she is deep in thought.

"I like you, Ella," she continues. "I think you're good for my brother. I don't know how much Cian has told you, but he wasn't always the sensible one. He was wild for a few years, partying as a true Rockstar does. Fame, it can either make or break a person. Unless they have a focus, it's easy to get lost in the midst of it all. I see that you make Cian happy, and I am thankful he found you again; we all are."

That's the second time tonight Rosie's words have made me question my relationship with Cian. How much do I know about him? He is a good dad. I know underneath all those tattoos and hardened exterior, there's a man who is soft and romantic. He adores his mother and sister and treats his band members like family, too. But how much can you really know someone you've only known a few short months? I'm not talking about the version he shows the world but the vulnerable, honest, real, raw version. If I want to spend my life with this man, I need to dig deeper, peel away his layers, and find the man he really is, not the one everyone perceives him to be.

We arrive back at Cian's house and follow the voices that lead us to the kitchen. There they are. My boys. They're sitting side by side at the kitchen's island, engrossed in the jigsaw they're working on.

We stand in the doorway, just taking in the scene before us. Two heads of messy, onyx black hair, two tongues sticking out of their mouths in concentration.

Seeing them side by side like this always makes my heart pound. Croí is Cian's mini, in every way. I have noticed over the past few weeks; they even sleep the same. Flat on their backs with one arm folded under their heads.

They still haven't noticed Rosie and me, they're too engrossed in their little puzzle. I thank God every day that Cian stuck around to get to know his son. He took to fatherhood instantly; from the moment he met Croí, he poured his heart and soul into him. Seeing the love between them makes me fall for the tattooed man a little more.

Cian lifts his head from the jigsaw, and when his eyes meet mine, a cheeky grin lights his handsome face. "Welcome home, Angel." *Home, I like the sound of that.*

"Hi, Mom," Croí says, never lifting his head from his Transformer jigsaw.

"How did you girls get on today?" Cian asks.

Rosie launches into how we spent our afternoon and how it was interrupted by a certain drummer boy.

"When will those two ever get their sh... stuff together?" He glances at Croí to see if he caught that little slip. Cian has been trying to rein in the cursing. I don't know why; Croí has lived with Cassie all his life, and that girl has the mouth of a trucker.

"How was work?" I ask. I make my way around the island to kiss my son on the forehead.

Cian pulls me into his arms. "It was good; we laid down three full tracks for the new album. Mark was very pleased with the new material. You should come with us to the studio soon and check it out. Croí would love all those buttons." He smirks, wiggling his dark brows and making me giggle.

"Where is Mam? I thought she said she would be here," Rosie questions.

"She's gone to deal with Da; she'll be back shortly. Will you keep an eye on Croí? I need to talk to El about something."

She nods in understanding. The tone he just used makes me wary. Whatever he needs to tell me isn't good.

"Sure, take your time." She takes a seat beside Croí, while Cian leads me down the hall towards his office.

This is the one room in the house I haven't been in yet. It's just as beautiful as the rest. The wall on the right is decorated with dark wooden shelves. They are filled with records and books. On the left is a glass cabinet, housing all the awards and trophies from both the 4Clover years and Cian's school days. His desk sits in the centre of the room; it's made from the same dark wood as the shelves. The wall behind the desk holds framed albums; I notice they're all 4Clover.

Cian leans back on the desk and crosses his arms over his chest. He takes a big breath inward then slowly blows it out.

"Come here, sit down." I know from his voice, whatever he needs to say is serious.

I make my way over to the leather armchair that's placed in front of Cian's desk. When I sit, he kneels in front of me taking my hands in his. "Ella, there is no easy way for me to say this... when I first found out about Croí, I had Lily dig into all the old band emails and phone calls. It had nothing to do with me not believing you. I just had to find out who would keep something so vital from me."

He runs his thumbs over the soft skin of my fingers before continuing, "I needed to know who on my band's payroll could be so cold as to keep a son from his father. When we arrived back in Ireland a few days ago, Lily handed me a folder. It contained every email you sent, every phone call you made. Every picture you sent of Croí over the years. There was also a USB stick with every voicemail you left — "

The tears fall from my eyes. I remember every time I tried to reach Cian. Those first few months were the worst of my life. I screamed, begged, and cried in those voicemails. I called him horrible things. I was a broken twenty-year-old with no one to lean on. Every year on Croí's birthday, I would post a package to Sham-Rock Records, containing a year's worth of photos of Croí. I documented every important event in his life. I never really gave up. Deep down, I knew those photos would end up in Cian's hands, eventually.

"Please, Angel, don't cry. I am here now, and I'm not going anywhere, okay?" He gently wipes the falling tears from my cheeks. "The reason I want to talk to you about this is, found out who was behind hiding any trace of you and Croí."

My eyes lock on his. This is hard for him; I can see the struggle in his stormy eyes. Finally, he takes a deep breath." It was my Dad, Ella." Cian's eyes hold a sadness that I've never seen in them before. "I need you to know, no matter what happens, I will never allow that man to be involved with you, or my son. He lost the right to be Croí's grandfather the moment he decided he would keep you both from me. I am working with Cillian and the twins to buy his half of the label off him. He is no longer welcome in my company. Today, as a band, we all decided that we cannot trust him. I already own part of Sham-Rock records, I just need to come up with a plan to take the rest. The other lads will buy in if they have to."

I'm shocked. I can't even form words to reply. That man kept my son a secret. The same man who greeted me the day I arrived with a smile and a warm, fatherly hug. The same man who pretended that my son was welcome here. He acted like his new grandson was a gift, not something he had been hiding for six years. How could he? How could he keep his own son in the dark for all these years? My horror must be all over my face because Cian pulls me into his arms, whispering words of promise and safety.

"As long as I am alive, Ella, you will never have to be alone again. I lost you once. I promise you; I'm never letting you go."

Chapter Twenty-Three

Dangerous Woman by Ariana Grande

Cian

*E*lla is upset about the news of Da's involvement, and rightly so. The man welcomed her with open arms when she first arrived here. Now, she knows he was the one behind all her past efforts going unanswered, and it has cut her deeply.

I hold her in my arms as she cries; I have no idea how hard those first few years were for her. If I could, I would take away all the hurt and pain she felt.

"I'm sorry, Cian. I thought I had dealt with this, but knowing it was someone who has a blood tie to my son is shocking. How could he do that to you... to us?" She fights back her tears.

"Angel, listen to me." I lift her chin with my finger, latching her gaze to mine. "Let's not worry about my Da for now. He will get what's coming to him in good time. I have you and Croí back now. That's all that matters." I kiss her forehead and wipe away the moisture under her eyes.

"I love you," I assure her.

"I love you, too."

I take her hand in mine, and together we make our way back down the hall to Rosie and Croí. We find them snuggled up together in the family room, watching 'Inside Out.' Cassie is curled into the armchair. "Hey guys," she greets.

I settle on the opposite side of the couch. I pull Ella down into my lap and wrap my arms around her. "How was your day?" Ella directs towards Cassie.

"It was good, but I'm exhausted. I think I'll turn in. I just wanted to say hello before I went to bed." Cassie stands, stretching her arms above her head. She leans forward, kissing Croí on the cheek. "Night, monkey."

"Night, Aunt Cas."

Ella stands to hug her best friend, and I get this overwhelming need to pull her back into my arms; I need her close. I'm terrified the bomb I just dropped on her was too huge.

Somewhere, deep down, I fear it will make her run for the hills like she usually does. I hope I've shown her by now how much I want and need her in my life.

Rosie sends me a look, beginning one of our silent sibling conversations.

Stop worrying, she's not going anywhere.
How do you know that?
We talked. She loves you.

Good, because I love her too.

Rosie winks then turns her attention back to the T.V. We have always been good at knowing what the other is thinking. With the small age gap between us, we grew up close. It came in handy when we were teenagers. But lately, I've noticed my sister is more guarded; only allowing me to see what she wants me to see.

Ella climbs back onto my lap, and I finally settle down. Halfway through the movie, Ma comes barrelling through the front door. Her arms are full of takeaway bags from my favourite Chinese restaurant.

"I brought food; everyone up at the table," she shouts, marching her way through the sitting room and into the kitchen.

Judging by the look on her face, things didn't go too well with Da. I make a mental note to ask her about that tomorrow.

The dinner passes; Ma makes sure to keep the conversation light and cheery in front of little ears.

Croí fills any silence with news of his day with his Nana, telling Ella all about his trip to the swimming pool. The smile on Ella's face seeing her son so happy warms my heart.

Before long, Ella rests her head against my

shoulder, hiding her yawn behind the palm of her hand.

It wouldn't take a genius to see she is drained, both mentally and physically.

"Why don't you head up and have a shower? I can get the little man to bed," I offer.

"You sure?" she questions, her eyes hazy with the need for sleep.

"Go, relax. I've got this." I place a chaste kiss against her plump lips. "I'll be right up."

"Night, everyone."

"Night, sweetheart," my mom replies with a wide smile.

|***|

Croí rushes up the stairs ahead of me; by the time I reach his room, he is under the covers with his new Nintendo switch glued to his face. Ella protested at how much I spoil him, but I missed so much of his life, I want to make up for it. Sure, buying him gifts probably isn't the way to go about it, but I can't help it. It makes him happy.

"Hey, buddy. What did your mom say about using electronics in bed?" I tease.

"Sorry, Dad." He quickly turns it off, placing it on the locker beside his bed. He lays his little head against the dinosaur pillowcase, and I tuck the matching duvet around him. "Can you read me a story?"

I'll read you twenty, as long as you're happy.

"Sure. One story, then it's time to sleep, okay?"

He claps with excitement. "Yes, I promise."

I read him his favourite story. It's called 'The Farting Dinosaur.' Of course, Croí thinks the word fart is hilarious, so before long he is laughing his head off.

We finish the book, and I turn on his night light. "Night, buddy. See you in the morning." I stand to leave, but his sleepy voice calls me back.

"Dad?"

"Yeah, little man?"

His blue eyes turn serious; there is something in them, I have never seen before. *Sadness.* "Are you going to marry my mommy?"

That question puts a smile on my face. I walk back over to his bed and sit down beside him. This is something I've been meaning to ask him, so I'm glad he was the one who brought it up.

"Hopefully. Would that be okay with you?"

His face lights up. "Yes! Cause if you marry my mom, I'll get to live here with you forever. I like it here. I don't want to go back to our little house. I want to stay here... with you.

I don't want you to go back either.

"I'd like that too, buddy. I'll see what I can do. Now go to sleep. I'll see you in the morning." I kiss his head and make my way to the master bedroom.

Looks like it's time to beg Ella to stay.

I enter the bedroom, and I'm greeted with the sound of the en-suite shower running. Ella's humming softly.

She left the door slightly ajar, a silent invitation for me to join her. I push open the door and stare at the beautiful goddess before me. She is facing the wall, giving me the perfect view of her round ass. I watch as the water runs down the curve of her spine. *What I would give to be that droplet of water.*

Ella is gorgeous, even in her everyday leggings, oversized t-shirts and converse — she calls them her Mom clothes — she is still the most beautiful woman I've ever laid my eyes on.

I stand there in awe, scanning every inch of her naked body into my memory.

She has an amazing figure; thanks to years of dancing, she's curvy in all the right places. Her skin is toned and tanned from the years living under the Californian sun.

Ella throws her head back, running her long brown hair under the water. She must sense me watching her like a creepy stalker because she turns to face me.

"Are you going to stand there creeping all night, Irish? Or are you going to strip off and join me?" she teases, running her hands over her soapy body.

I don't need to be told twice. I strip off my clothes quicker than Channing Tatum and step into the double-headed walk-in shower.

The shower is probably my favourite thing about this whole house — grey slate tiles with a double-headed rain shower and triple wall jets on either side — even more so now that Ella is standing in it.

I pull her body close, resting her back against my

chest. I take the cloth from her hand and begin to wash her breasts in a circular motion. I move in slow torturous strokes, barely brushing against her nipples. A throaty moan escapes her lips, sending my dick into overdrive.

Ever so slowly, I run the cloth over her tightly toned stomach. Her back arches.

"Cian." My name falls from her lips in a needy whimper. Her head falls back to rest on my shoulder, leaving her neck exposed to me. I trail my lips over the space between her ear and collarbone, placing small kisses in my wake. Goosebumps erupt along her skin.

I drop the cloth against the shower base and run my fingers through her folds. "What's got you so wet, Angel? Me or the shower?"

"It's the shower," she teases, her voices airy from how turned on she is.

I pull my hand away from her promise land and she whimpers in protest.

"What's that, baby?"

"You... you make me wet." She grabs my hand placing it back where she needs it most.

"That's what I thought," I whisper against her neck. I tease her clit with my fingers before spinning her around and pressing her up against the wall. Her arms wrap around my neck. I lift her leg with my left hand and plunge two fingers into her with my right.

"Oh, God!" I circle her clit with my thumb while curling my fingers inside her depth, rubbing against her G-spot with each stroke.

In a matter of seconds, her body shakes in my arms. "Oh, God, Cian. Yes."

She rides out her orgasm, her inner walls tightening around my fingers. Once she has come down, a wicked look appears in her eyes. "My turn," she demands.

She takes my body wash from the built-in shelf and squeezes some into her soft hands. She starts by rubbing the gel across my chest. Her hands slowly glide down the hard ridges of my stomach, towards the deep v that leads to my very erect penis.

My breath hitches in my chest as she wraps her two hands around my full length. She pumps my cock, once, twice, then she lowers herself onto her knees. *Fuck, she's going to be the death of me.*

"Ella," I moan out as she runs her tongue from base to tip. She looks up at me through her thick, black lashes; as she slowly traces over the sensitive head, her eyes never leave mine.

My body jerks at the sensations she's creating. She torturously wraps her mouth around my engorged cock, taking me in inch by inch, until I'm hitting the back of her throat.

"Sweet Jesus, Angel." I grip her hair between my fingers, fighting against the urge to fuck her pretty mouth harder.

She moans in reply, sending shivers straight up my shaft. Her hand grips my ass, forcing my dick deeper into her mouth. My God! I tug her hair a little harder, pumping my hips. She quickens her pace, using both her hands and mouth. I swear I see stars as my seed spills down her throat.

"Fuck me, woman." I breathe out, trying to catch my breath.

She stands to her full height, running her fingers nails over my eight pack.

"Oh, I intend to," she says with a wink.

Chapter Twenty-Four

Ella

I've quickly come to the realization that lying in Cian's arms is one of the best feelings in the world. After our shower, we headed straight to bed, where Cian worshipped my body for hours on end. He left no part untouched. I have never felt so satisfied, so loved, so cherished in my entire life. But even so, somewhere in the back of my mind, I'm waiting for the penny to drop. There is no way a man can be as perfect as he is.

The glow of the moon shines through the skylight, lighting up the bed where we lie. There is a comfortable silence between us as Cian's fingers slowly trace up and down my stomach.

I want to ask him how we will work this.

Surely, this happy family we're playing can't last forever. There are just way too many variables.

His career and the fame that comes with it. All those women who would give their left tit to sleep with him. I don't know how I would deal with that. Not well, that's for sure. Then there is the fact we live an ocean apart. Oh, and let's not forget the minor detail of his dad hating me. We have been so caught up in our little love bubble we have avoided the main obstacles that could potentially ruin us.

Cian must sense my change in mood; his arm tightens around my waist, pulling my back closer to his chest. "What's wrong, Angel?"

"Just thinking." I release a heavy sigh and turn to face him. He looks so handsome right now. The light of the moon glistens against his face, highlighting his chiselled jawline and high cheekbones. Why does he have to look so sexy all the damn time?

"Talk to me, Ella. Tell me what's wrong." He kisses my forehead, and when he pulls back, his eyes hold a hint of sadness.

I decide it's time to pull up my metaphorical big-girl-panties and just come out with it. "I know we said we would put this conversation on hold, but Rosie's wedding is fast approaching, and I just..."

I drag in a deep breath through my nose, blowing it out my mouth. I swallow back the lump in my throat, forcing myself to continue.

"I need to know what is going on here, Cian. I need a plan. Every day I fall in love with you a little more." I cup his cheek within my palm, locking his eyes to mine. "I just don't want to be left broken when reality comes and smacks me in the face."

Cian pushes himself up. He sits back against the

headboard and pulls me in close. He wraps me up in his arms, so my head can rest in the nook where his shoulder meets his neck.

"I want to talk about this too. The last few days, it's been playing on my mind. I just didn't know how to bring it up without being a controlling bastard." He runs his tattooed fingers through my hair, bringing me the comfort I need. "The truth is, Ella, I don't want you to leave. I want you to stay here with me. You and Croí. I feel like we have lost so much time already." His words fill my heart. I want that too.

"I know you are independent, and that you don't want to rely on me, but it's just money, Ella. Everything I own belongs to you too. It's yours and it's our son's." I tilt my chin so I can see his beautiful face. He is saying everything I've ever wanted him to.

"If you are hellbent on working, there are plenty of jobs you can do here. If that's what you really want. 4Clover are always looking for dancers for music videos, and Lily can help you look for something else if that doesn't appeal." He runs his thumb across my bottom lip. His eyes are shining; the way he looks at me is full of love and adoration.

"Isabella Andrews, I want you in my life. I know it's asking a lot. You would have to pack up your life and move halfway across the world, but if you just give me... us a chance, I promise you, I will do my best every day to make sure you never have a single ounce of doubt in my love for you and our son.

I want you to stay. This house, it's not a home. Not without my family in it." Relief flows through me and happy tears fall from my eyes. He wants us. His family.

I want to stay. I really do, but what if our love isn't enough to withstand the pressure that comes with loving a Rockstar?

"What about your job, Cian? What happens when it's time for you to go back on tour?

How do we handle the media shitstorm that's bound to come when they find out about Croí?

Not to mention, the tension between you and your dad.

I know it's a lot of questions, but we need to figure this out."

I know I sound like a negative Nancy, but as much as I love him, we need to work this out. I can't uproot Croí and my life without some sort of plan. It's not only my heart on the line here. I'm a Mom, I need to think of how this will affect Croí too.

"I won't lie to you. My job is tough. We can be gone for months at a time. Ideally, I would love you and Croí to come with me. If you do, we can school him on the road, and I'll get to show you both the world. At the moment, we are only working on the next album, and we do that here in Dublin in Ciaran's home studio."

"Okay, so you're based here for a few months?" I ask.

"Yeah, the tour won't begin until next summer at the earliest, so we have plenty of time to narrow down the details. And as for my dad, well, he will just have to get used to this. He doesn't have a say.

This is between the two of us and the son we share." He takes my hand in his, bringing it towards his lips. He kisses my knuckles, one by one.

"At the moment, I can't forget what he did. He chose money over my happiness, and to me, that is unforgivable. I can't even look at him right now without wanting to kill him. He has burned bridges with all of us — me, Rosie, Mam, Cillian and even the twins." He looks so torn up. I never really had a relationship with my father, but it's clear to see, once upon a time Cian idolized his.

"Over the years, my Da turned into a brutal man, only out for his own gain. What he did to us, well that was the final straw. You don't need to worry about him anymore. I will deal with him when the time is right. I will hit him where it hurts the most: his bank account. It might take a while, but he'll get what he deserves."

"And Croí and the media?" I question. This is the one I'm most anxious about. I don't want my baby caught up in all this.

Cian squeezes his eyes tight. I know he's worried about this too, and just like me, he has no control over it. "That... is a different ball game; even if you decide to leave, Ella, they'll find out about you, eventually. The best thing we can do is beat them to it." What does that mean?

Cian must hear my silent question because he answers like he knows exactly what I was thinking. "We tell the world that we are together, then after Rosie's wedding, we can hold a press conference. Tell them the truth about you and Croí. That way, they can't catch us off guard, and the ball will be in our court. There is no way around the papers; they're vultures and won't stop until they find a story worth telling. Once they see we are in this for the long haul... they'll move on."

Cian pulls me up into his lap so I'm straddling him. He takes my face between his hands, and his eyes find mine.

"Stay. For me. For us. I know there's going to be some rough times, but together, we'll get through them. I can't promise you we won't face any storms, but I can promise the calm we have together will be worth it. I want this. I want you. I will do whatever it takes to make this work." He pushes the strands of hair that escaped my mom-bun behind my ear. His eyes never leave mine, not for a second. He captures my lips with his; kissing me with a passion so fierce it erases all my doubt.

He pulls back and gazes into my eyes with an intensity that reaches my soul. "I want to dream with you, build my life with you. I want to look out at the crowd and see you there cheering me on.

I want to encourage you to achieve all your goals and dreams. I want you to show me all your imperfections, the parts of yourself that you don't love, just so I can love them enough for the both of us. From the moment I saw you, Ella, my soul recognized you.

You are the other half of me. I will not let you walk away from this, from us. Not without one hell of a fight. I love you. Now and for the rest of my life. So please, Angel. Say you'll stay."

Tears stream down my cheeks at his declaration. This man loves me with all he has. We can do this; we can make this work.

"Okay. Yes. I'll stay."

"Thank-fucking-God," he shouts before he flips me over onto my back and shows me all over again how much he loves me — this time with his tongue.

Chapter Twenty-Five

Cian

I've been pacing back and forth over the oak floorboards of my office for the past half an hour. The shelf covered walls are closing in around me while all the air in the room dissipates. A whirlwind of emotion brews under the surface of my skin, as I force each breath in through my nose and out heavily through my mouth in order to calm the rapid beating of my heart.

This morning — *fuck*. This morning, I was the happiest man in Ireland. I woke to the softness of the woman I love, treasured tightly within my arms. Our satin sheets covered her naked body, caressing her golden skin the same way my hands did the night before. I was in a state of pure perpetual bliss.

Now, not so much. My world *as I know it* has been pulled from underneath my feet. It came crashing down, crumbling to rubble around me. My heart and all its broken shards left in pieces among the debris.

Deep down, I'm thankful that Croí is spending the night with Rosie and that Cassie and Conor are working on new artwork for the upcoming album cover. Because Ella and I need to talk.

I rub the heel of my hands over my eyes as I blow out a heavy sigh. *How did I get to this?* One minute, I'm checking emails while Ella makes us dinner, and the next, I'm firing my laptop across the room, watching in slow motion as it explodes against the sage green wall.

My body sinks to the floor, and I rest my head back against my desk. I stay there, just staring up at the ceiling, every moment I've spent with Ella and Croí running through my mind like an old movie reel. My shoulders shake as a flood of tears escape my eyes. *Fuck, fuck, fuck.*

I reach for my iPhone in my back pocket. I pull up my emails. I need to see it again, read it again.

I click on the last email Lily sent.

Subject: Whatever you do, DO NOT JUMP TO CONCLUSIONS!
<Lily-thebossbitch-O'Shea@ 4Clover.ie>

Cian,
Why the hell are you not answering your phone? I've been calling you all afternoon. This is my last attempt before I come barrelling through your house like a bat out of the gates of hell. (I SHIT YOU NOT.)

I've attached an article released today by Starz Weekly. Please, DO NOT jump to conclusions. Read it, talk to Ella, (CALMLY) and let me know how you want to proceed. My phone has been ringing all day; they want a comment. I know you were trying to keep this under the radar until after Rosie's wedding. But, it's out now, and I think we need to shut it down before it grows legs. Again, DO NOT JUMP TO CONCLUSIONS!
Lily 'THE BOSS BITCH' O'Shea.

I press the small attachment icon and relive the moment that tore my heart out. I re-read it over and over. My eyes travel over every letter of the published article in my hands. With every ink printed word, my heart aches a little more. Everything I once believed in... I now question. *How? How could she do this to me?*

Starz Weekly

Last week, women all over the world nursed their broken hearts when the tattooed, lead singer of 4Clover posted a selfie on his Instagram, officially announcing his relationship. The image was of him, cuddled up with a gorgeous brunette. The photo captioned: Forever&Always. #mysoul #mylove #myluck #myoneandonly

The pair have been spending a lot of time together in recent weeks. They were spotted leaving Los Angeles' five-star restaurant, BLU, back in September, and again, roaming the streets of Dublin as early as last week.

For weeks, we have all been wondering, who is the brunette that has been seen — on many occasions — on

Irish Rockstar Cian Mulligan's arm?

Well, ladies and gentlemen, today is your lucky day.

Isabella May Andrews, 27, is an "exotic dancer" at The DollHouse. TDH is known as Los Angeles' most Elite Gentlemen's Club. Our first thought was, Cian met her there while attending a bachelor party in early September. But, with some further investigating, we found out Ella Andrews met the singer in the very early years of his music career. 4Clover was performing at a local student bar — where Ella attended college — for a Valentine's Day event. We have been led to believe the couple had a rendezvous that night. Croí Andrews, Ella's son, was born nine months after the couple's first encounter, arousing speculations that Cian could be, in fact, the young boy's father.

But, is Cian Mulligan really the father? Or, is there a possibility that little Croí belongs to Ella's dark-haired, blue-eyed ex-boyfriend, Jake Saunders?

We received a call this week from Jake Saunders, who claims he was Ella's college sweetheart. He informed us that he and Ms. Andrews were still very much together around the time of the child's conception.

They had been seeing each other for around six months, and he was devastated when he found out that Ella had slept with the sexy tattooed singer, ultimately putting an end to their relationship.

"I loved her; we had made plans for the future. I was heartbroken when I heard of her infidelity," he said.

When we asked him if he knew anything about Ella and her son, he replied, "**No, the last time I saw Ella was on campus, about three months after our break-**

up. She was acting weird. It seemed like she couldn't get away from me quick enough. The first I heard about the kid was last week. Immediately, alarm bells sounded in my head. We had been intimate right up to the end of our relationship. I calculated the timeline, and I believe the kid could be mine, not Cian's."

Oh, juicy stuff!

So, who is Ella Andrews? We dug a little deeper into her past and several sources say: she had a rough life. Her mother died when she was a small child, and she was left in the care of her Grandmother — who passed away from cancer just months before Ella got pregnant with her son. At the news of her pregnancy, the dark-haired college beauty was forced to drop her classes at UCLA. Later, she began working nights as a dancer at the prestigious men's club, earning just enough money to provide for her son.

What we think is: The college dropout turned exotic dancer saw an opportunity to pin the paternity of her son on the multi-platinum singer to alleviate her financial burdens.

What do you think? Did Ms. Andrews concoct this plan? Has she finally managed to make Cian Mulligan fall for her tricks? Our sources tell us the couple is currently playing happy families in Cian's countryside home in North County Dublin. SO, WE THINK... Yes!

So, our trusted readers, we ask you... who is the Daddy?

Ella

I love this kitchen; it is the perfect mix of modern meets old Irish country. The contemporary appliances fit seamlessly alongside the nostalgic detail. The warm white glass-front cabinets are accentuated by the soft sage green walls. The deep farmhouse sink is big enough to bathe in and don't get me started on the large range stove. Rosie really did an amazing job designing this space. She highlighted the country style by adding baskets, blue canning jars, and vintage ceramics. *Did I say I was in love with this kitchen?*

I draw in a deep breath, and the aroma of the homemade Guinness stew I am brewing fills my nose. I called Maggie earlier and asked her what Cian's favourite meal was.

She told me to grab a pen and paper, and once I was all set, she rattled off her grandmother's age-old recipe. I'm looking forward to trying the traditional Irish dish because it smells delicious. I turn off the gas, leaving the stew to simmer and make my way down the hallway towards Cian's home office.

"Cian." I knock.

After no answer, I twist the handle and push open the door. I'm not prepared for the sight before me. Cian is sitting on the floor, his back pressed to his wooden desk. His legs are pulled tightly to his wide chest. His face is buried against his knees, his onyx hair pointing in all directions.

I rush to his side, dropping to the floor beside him. "Baby, what's wrong?" I say, rubbing my hand over his spine. He turns his head to the side, refusing to look at me. *What the hell is going on?*

"Cian. Please, look at me. Tell me what's going on." I've never seen him like this, so... tortured. Panic takes over. I reach out, I place my hand against his cheek and when he pulls away at my touch, my heart aches.

"Don't touch me. I can't have you near me right now." He pulls his lower lip between his teeth and curls his hand into a fist, resting under his chin.

"Cian, please. Tell me what happened. What did I do?" I beg through my falling tears.

He has never spoken to me like this before. So full of anger and hate. This is a side of Cian I'm not used to.

I sit there for a moment, pleading with my eyes for him to open up to me. Finally, he slides his phone towards me across the floorboards. "Read that," he demands, his tone full of disgust.

I reach for the phone with a shaky hand. I scroll down until I reach the part where Jake gives his interview and my anger builds. He was always a pretentious prick, but this is low, even for his standards. I rack my brain for any reason he would want to go to the press. I haven't spoken to him in years. What could he possibly get from this? Then like a light switch that's been flicked on, it hits me... money. He did it for money.

"Cian, I can explain, I — "

"Is it true?" he interrupts. This is the first time he has looked at me since I entered his office. The hurt in his eyes is building, clouding over like a storm brewing beyond the horizon.

"No, not all of it," I force out with a harboured breath.

"Which-fucking-part is? Fuck, probably all of it. I don't know." He waves his hands in front of his face, making his aggravation evident.

"Is Croí mine, Ella?" he asks with a murderous expression.

"Of course, he — "

"Really? How can you be so fucking sure? Your boyfriend at the time seems to think differently."

"He was not my boyfriend; we had broken up. If you would just let me expl — "

"Did he know that?" he throws in my face, cutting off my sentence.

"Of course, he did. I caught him with his face buried between some chick's legs. I think it was implied, and if it wasn't, I told him as much at the bar that night."

Cian moves to stand inches from my face, his six-foot-four frame towering over me. I stand to match him. *Your intimidation won't work here, Irish.*

"You're telling me, you broke up with your boyfriend hours before we slept together, yet you're one hundred percent sure that the little boy I have fallen in love with is mine? I find that hard to believe."

Rage boils beneath my skin. How dare he question me? I am not the kind of person he is making me out to be. I would never lie about this, about the paternity of my son. If he can take the word of the press over mine, what does that say for our relationship? *Not very much.* He is Croí's father. That much I'm sure of. If he just gave me a chance to explain, I could tell him that. I decided if he doesn't want to believe me, well, that's on him.

"Do you know what, Cian. Fuck you. That boy is yours. Of that I am certain. Believe whatever you want. I'm out of here." I turn on my heel and head for the door.

"Where are you going?" he demands.

"Somewhere you're fucking not." I grab my purse, phone, and coat from the kitchen and march out the front door. Finally, I allow myself to break fully.

Chapter Twenty-Six

Hollow by James Smith

Ella

*W*hat am I going to do now? I'm in a foreign country with nowhere to go. Do you know what? I don't care. I couldn't spend another minute in that house with Cian.

I take a seat on the stone wall at the end of the too-long driveway and take a moment to try and gather myself, not that it makes any difference.

I'm speechless with anger; molten rage flooding my veins. I can't even begin to dissect what just happened in Cian's office. How could he take the word of the press at face value? He didn't even give me a chance to speak, to explain. What happened to *we're a team, Ella?* He is so full of shit; as soon as things got rough, he just gave up. I feel so stupid; everything he ever said, all the things he promised, it was all an illusion. I was so caught up in our fairy-tale romance, I never once thought he would question us and our relationship.

I pull my phone from my purse, dialling Cassie's number. *Pick up, pick up.* "Hi, you've reached Cassie,

213 | P a g e

leave a message." *Shit!*

"Cas, where are you? Cian and I had a fight. I need you." I end the call, and the panic creeps in. I scroll through my contacts until I reach Rosie's number; I hit dial and wait for her to pick up.

"Hey, Hun. Is everything okay? I wasn't expecting to hear from you, at least not until the morning." Her cheery tone only makes me feel worse. When I don't respond, she adds, "El, are you there?"

"Rosie." I sniff, pushing back the tears threatening to fall.

"What did he do?" She immediately blames Cian. "It was that stupid article, wasn't it?"

"Yeah, can... can you come and get me? I... I just can't be here right now," I plead, pouring my broken heart down the phone line. I hate putting her in this position. Cian is her family, her blood. I don't want to cause tension between them. But Croí is there, and right now, I just need to hold him.

"Of course, I'll get Lily to watch Croí. Hold tight, I'll be right there." She ends the call and I sit back and wait. I stare up at the blackened sky; the moon is reflecting its light, but I can't see it. The events that have transpired have covered me in darkness.

"Nana, I need you. Everything is a mess."

The words of that stupid article run through my mind repeatedly.

The college dropout turned exotic dancer saw an opportunity to pin the paternity of her son on the multi-platinum singer to alleviate her financial burdens.

What a bunch of assholes. I despise this, the picture they painted of me. And, even more so, I hate the fact Cian believes it. I'm so angry at him, but I'm also hurt. All the things he said over the past few months seem worthless now, just words with no substance.

I rest my head in the palm of my hands and wait, letting the tears fall to the gravel beneath my feet. I'm not sure we can fix this, and after the way Cian reacted, I'm not sure he wants to.

|***|

"El, can I come in?" Rosie's head peeks into her spare bedroom through the small opening of the door.

"Yeah, sure." I keep my voice low careful not to wake Croí, who is fast asleep cradled in my arms. I gently remove my arm from under him, tucking him in tight under the blanket.

"Goodnight, little man," I whisper to Croí before walking towards Rosie. She stands by the door, watching me closely like she's afraid that if she takes her eyes off me, I'll run.

"Lily opened some wine. Do you fancy a glass?" she offers. On the drive from Cian's, Rosie didn't pressure me to talk, which I'm thankful for, but the look on her porcelain face portrays she wants answers. I suck in a deep breath. I knew this was coming, and if I'm going to explain everything to them, wine is needed.

"Yeah, sure." I click off the bedside lamp and follow her back to the living room.

I make myself comfortable on the large cuddle chair; I drape one of Rosie's chunky grey knits throws over my body and reach for the glass of wine Lily is holding out for me.

"I suppose you want answers," I break the heavy silence.

"Only if you want to," Lily assures. "We all have a story, El. Whether you want to share it, well, that is up to you."

"I have a question," Rosie finally speaks up. "I don't want you to take this the wrong way, but Cian is my brother, and I would do anything for him. So, I have to ask." She leans forward, placing her hand on top of mine. "Whatever answer you give; I will not dispute. I'll take you at your word." I know what she is going to ask, and honestly, I don't blame her. "Is Croí Cian's son, Ella?"

"Yes." I lock my eyes to hers, confident in my answer. "I had a DNA test done."

I swallow back the lump in my throat. "After Croí was born, I knew Cian was his dad, but somewhere in the back of my mind, there was a pinprick of doubt. I wanted to be certain." I lift my wine glass to my lips, washing the sandpaper dryness from my mouth. "I couldn't get a hold of Cian, as you know I tried, relentlessly. I had only ever slept with two people, Jake and Cian. So, the only option I had was to rule one out."

I shift in the chair, remembering just how

difficult that time of my life was. Lily and Rosie both sit in silence allowing me to speak, which I'm thankful for. "The night I met Cian; I had just broken up with my boyfriend. I found him with some other girl." I hear Lily cringe and mutter something along the lines of, asshole.

"Jake and I, we always used protection. So, the chances of him being Croí's dad were slim. The night I was with Cian, we were so caught up in each other that using protection never crossed my mind. Stupid, I know. Anyway, after I couldn't contact Cian, Cassie suggested getting Jake to take the test. That way I could be one hundred percent."

I push by the turmoil the past brings. "At first, I didn't want to involve Jake, but then more time passed without a word from Cian. Croí was getting bigger by the day, and I knew if Cian was his father, I wanted Croí to know him, know who his dad was. So, I pulled up my proverbial big girl pants and paid Jake a visit." I stand from the chair, walking out the nervous energy building beneath my skin.

"I hadn't seen him since I'd left college so, naturally, when he opened the door and saw the baby I was cradling, his jaw hit the floor." I release a pathetic laugh recalling the look on Jake's face when I knocked on his dorm room door with a four-month-old Croí, strapped to my chest. "The first thing he said was, '*That better not be mine.*' I remember wanting to smack the look of disgust off his face."

"I would have," Lily interjects, raising her glass to

her lips.

"Me too," Rosie adds.

"If I hadn't got Croí with me, I would have. Anyway, after finally convincing him to speak to me, I managed to get him to agree to take the test under his terms."

"Which were?" Rosie asks from her spot on the couch.

"I had to pay him two-thousand-dollars, and if the results came back that he was Croí's dad, I would not fight him for support. We agreed that if he was the father, he would sign over all rights to Croí, solely to me. He wanted no part of it, and in my naive mind, I agreed. A few days later, he took the test."

"You paid him? How?" Lily questions doing nothing to hide her shock. I raise my brows in answer. "I took the money from the inheritance my Nana left me."

I was desperate for answers. This is also the reason why I wasn't surprised to see he went to the press; he's always been a money-hungry asswipe. He saw an opportunity to make a quick buck, and he took it.

"For weeks, I checked my mailbox four or five times a day. I was like an anti-Christ. I don't know why; I knew deep down Croí was Cian's, but I needed that piece of paper like I needed my next breath. The day they came, I couldn't open them. I was terrified; the what if's started to creep in, pulling me under. How was I going to look after my precious baby all by myself? Cassie stood by me; she promised me no matter what was in that envelope, she would be there to help me get through it."

"I'm glad you had her," Rosie offers.

"Yeah, she was great. Together we opened that letter. One sentence stood out amongst the rest." I recite the words I read a thousand times. "The results indicate that the alleged father is not the biological father of the child in question." I never felt relief like I did that day. The weight I had been carrying around for months lifted off my shoulders with that one sentence. "I texted Jake that evening, letting him know he was off the hook. He was not the father. He sent me a *yay hands emoji* and that was it. I haven't spoken to him since."

I take my seat and turn to face Rosie. "So, yes. To answer your question, Cian is one-hundred percent Croí's father."

Cian

I walk the empty rooms. They're lifeless without their presence — a shell of a house that needs them in it to make it a home. I fight off the memories of her that consume me like a fire, spreading over my skin and engulfing me within the flames. The space in my chest where my heart used to be is now replaced with tiny fragments of glass, causing a pain that is indescribable. People say heartbreak is a scar on your heart, but scars are wounds that have healed. What I feel is more of an eternal bleed, the hurt trapped beneath my skin with nowhere to go, tender to touch, like a bruise.

I can't believe she just left. Granted, I didn't really let her speak, but what did she expect; I had just found out I could be living a lie. Right now, I feel as if I'm seated on a seesaw of emotion, tipping back and forth between heartbreak and anger. I'm struggling to find balance.

The information I received from that article is putting untold pressure on my mind, and I'm seconds from combusting. I don't know what to do.

I stumble down the hallway, a bottle of Jameson in my hand. I run my fingertips across the frames that line the wall. I stop at the new addition Cassie gave me last week. A large black frame that holds six four-by-six photographs. I suppress the urge to rip it off the wall. Each photograph is a reminder of what might not be mine. *A family: a father who loves his son, a woman who loves a man, a boy who idolizes them both.*

My solar plexus tightens as my body shakes. Tears fall from my eyes, mourning for the life I thought I could have. I force my feet to move, and I lift the bottle to my lips, allowing the burn from the liquor to chase away some of my pain.

I continue down the hallway until I reach Croí's room. My eyes scan the newly painted walls.

The cobalt blue colour mocks me. I step in further. The large mural wall painting of Optimus

Prime and Bumblebee — that Rosie spent all last week painting — stares back at me from behind the head of Croí's bed. I wanted this to be his space, a place he could call his own. I recall how his face lit up when I told him he could decorate it however he liked.

"Can I have a transformer room? Can I, Dad, can I?" *Excitement radiates from every cell of his body.*

"Of course, you can buddy. You can have whatever you want." I rub my knuckles over his black hair, making him laugh. "Aunt Rosie will help you look through some transformer rooms online, and you can pick whichever one you like, okay?"

"Yay, best day ever," he shouts like he hasn't said that about every day he's been here.

A wave of sadness floods my throat. I swallow it down with another mouthful of amber liquid. I place the bottle on top of the dressing table and move to the bed. I lay on top of the duvet allowing Croí's scent to fill my nose. *Please be mine, please be my boy.*

I don't know the exact amount of time I lay there. Could be minutes, could be hours; either way, it didn't bring them back. The room is dark, but with the Irish evenings being so short this time of year, it could be any time after seven-o-clock.

A shadowed figure lurks in the door, illuminated by the light in the hallway.
"Hey, man. You're a little on the large side to be sleeping in that bed." Typical Ciaran, always trying to lighten the mood. Unfortunately for him, I'm not

in the humour.

"What are you doing here?" I question. I sit up in the bed, rubbing the moisture from my eyes. I clutch Croí's teddy bear in my hands. *I miss him. I miss them both.*

"I was at Lily's when Rosie and Ella landed back at their place. She was in a bad way, man. What happened?" He strides into the room in true Ciaran fashion. He lifts the bottle of Jameson off the dresser and takes a seat beside me.

"I see we are hitting the hard stuff," he adds. He brings the bottle to his lips, swallowing back a mouthful.

"What do you want, Maguire?"

"Well, that's just rude. I came to see if you were okay." He shakes the bottle in my face. "Luckily, I did. 4Clover already has its designated alcoholic; we don't need another."

I pull the booze from his grip. "Don't worry, Princess. I won't make it a habit; it's just been a rough day."

"Do you want to talk it out? Share our feelings and all that other manly shit?" Ciaran pouts, giving me his best impression of puppy dog eyes.

"Nope." I release a sigh. "It's just I — "

"I thought you said you didn't want to talk about it," he interrupts.

"Would you just shut up and listen?" I bark.

"Okay, sorry. But, can we go somewhere else? Optimus Prime is staring at me and he's giving me the creeps."

"You're a dick." I throw Croí's pillow at his head.

Ciaran stands and walks from the room in the direction of the kitchen. "That's Mr. Big Dick to you." *Asshole.*

|***|

"This stew is fucking delicious," Ciaran moans, scooping another mouthful of the dinner Ella made before she left into his mouth.

I take a seat on the far side of the counter. "I'm glad you're enjoying it," I announce with a hint of sarcasm.

"So, tell me, what happened? Why are you here looking about as miserable as a wet Irish summer day?"

I show him the article and sit silently as he reads it. I try to gauge his reaction from his facial expressions but come up with nothing. When he's finished reading, he slides the phone across the counter. He lifts his spoon to his mouth without a word. *Say something, for fuck's sake.*

"Well?" I encourage.

He sits back in his stool, folding his arms across his chest. "You're an idiot," he states like it's the only conclusion he can come up with.

"What?"

"Let me ask you something, Cian." He leans forward, glaring at me from his side of the kitchen island. "How long are we in the business?

"Six, seven years, give or take."

"And, how many times during that time did the papers, magazines, and the radio stations release a story about one of us that was complete and utter bollox?" *Too fucking-many.*

"Did you even give Ella a chance to speak?" he pushes. I stare at him blankly.

"Judging by your face, I'm thinking no. So, as I said. You're an idiot."

"But... she had a boyfriend; Croí could be his. We both have dark hair and blue eyes."

"Okay, I take it back, you're a blind idiot." he offers, before digging back into what was meant to be my dinner. He fills his face with two more mouthfuls then continues. "Look, man, I have zero doubt in my mind that the little dude is yours. He is your double. Jesus, Cian, he even walks like you. You have the same goddamn dimples. So, either you momentarily lost your mind or you're a blind idiot."

I take a moment to process his words. I picture Croí's face in my mind. From his shaggy black hair, his storm blue eyes with flecks of silvery grey around his irises. The cheeky, crooked smile that makes his dimples deepen. He is all me. There isn't a trace of Ella in him. *Shit.*

Ciaran pulls his leather wallet from his back pocket. He takes out an old photo, unfolding it and placing it before me. I stare down at the four boys in the picture. They must be about ten or so. I remember that day like it was only yesterday. He points at the boy in the centre, with his tongue sticking out at whoever took the photo. If you didn't know, you would swear that boy was Croí, but it's not. *It's me.*

"Tell me now, Cian. Who is Croí's dad?"

"I am." The tears fall again, but this time, they're happy tears.

"And what are you going to do about that?" he shouts like he's Oprah.

"Go get my family."

"YES! But first, you apologize with a side serving of grovelling."

"Maybe you're right."

"I always am. The sooner everyone realizes that the world will be a much brighter place."

Chapter Twenty-Seven

Ella

I've been twisting and turning on the double bed in the guest room of Lily and Rosie's house for the last two hours. No matter how many times I force myself to try and sleep, I can't. Every time I close my eyes, Cian's face stares back at me. I glance to my right, where Croí is sleeping peacefully. His messy hair is sticking up in all directions. A wave of sadness threatens to pull me under. *How do I explain this to him? He is just a kid.*

This was what I was most afraid of, Croí getting attached only to have the rug pulled from beneath him. Ever since Cian entered his life, he has been the happiest I've ever seen him, and now after everything that happened... I don't want to break his heart. *No mother wants that.*

I pull my phone from under my pillow and unlock it using my thumbprint. The light from the screen illuminates the dark bedroom. I open my safari browser, and even though I know I shouldn't, I google my name. *Isabella Andrews.*

Article after article fills my screen. Looks as though the media are having a field day at my expense. I knew this would happen; once one outlet releases information, the rest were sure to follow. I scroll down the long list of headlines, torturing myself a little more. They all hold the same information as the first, each one putting their own spin on it, but what really gets me are the comments from the public.

Cian, what the hell are you thinking? Butt ugly is too nice of a word to describe that sewer rat.

Ella Andrews is nothing but a gold-digging whore, hopefully, Cian sees sense.

I'd say that girl has more STDs than brain cells. That kid could be anyone's, she opens her legs for a living.

The poor kid looks dirty and malnourished, someone needs to contact CPS!!!

How can people be so hurtful, so cruel? Tears well up in my eyes and my body shakes as they silently fall. I slide from the bed, careful not to wake Croí, and with my phone in my hand, I head for the kitchen.

I'm filling a glass with water when the overhead light flicks on.

"Hey, couldn't sleep?" Cas questions from behind me. I turn to face her as she releases a yawn.

"Sorry, did I wake you?" I apologize. I move to the high stools around the breakfast island.

"No, I was awake. I heard you come down the hall." She enters the kitchen, flicking on the kettle. She leans against the counter and looks at me with sad eyes.

"How are you doing?" Her lips curl with concern.

"Not great. The articles are getting worse. I don't think I can live like this. They are tearing my life apart. How can any relationship last through this pressure?" I rub the heel of my palms against my brow line, trying to wipe away the stress headache building behind my eyes.

Cassie moves to the stool beside me. She runs her hand up and down my spine. "This is you and Cian; you can get through this," she assures.

I lift my head from my palms and lock my gaze to hers. "Can we though? You didn't see him earlier, Cassie. He jumped so far into conclusions, he got lost in them. He didn't give me a chance to explain. He had no faith in us. He questioned our relationship, he questioned Croí."

She nods her head in understanding. "So, what now?"

"I'm going home." I croak out. Leaving Ireland is the last thing I want to do, but right now, there is nothing here for me.

"Okay, I'll phone Conor in the morning and tell him he will have to hire another photographer for the artwork for the next tour," she states.

"No, you are not losing this opportunity because of me. Stay. Finish your job; you have put Croí and me ahead of yourself for too long. We will be okay; I just need time to figure this all out."

"El, I'm not going to stay here without you; you're my best friend. Where you go, I go. You're my person, remember?" Cassie bumps her shoulder off mine. "I love you, chic."

"I love you too, and that's why you have to stay. You deserve this, Cas. You are super talented; 4Clover are lucky to have you, and so am I. You can always visit me. Please stay, follow your dreams." I can see she is torn between staying and following her passion. "I've booked the tickets; we are leaving tomorrow night. There were only two seats available, so please, stay. If not for yourself, for me. I couldn't live with myself if you missed out on the career of a lifetime because of my mess."

She releases a weighted breath. "Okay, I'll stay, but only until I have this tour promo done. After that, I'm coming home. No fighting me, okay?"

"Okay," I agree. For now. There's no way I'm letting her throw this opportunity away.

"I spoke to Sam earlier," I add. "I asked her to swing by our house before her shift at The Dollhouse and send me a copy of the DNA results from my desk," I explain.

Cassie lifts her cup of tea to her lips letting me get everything out.

"I'm going to print them off tomorrow on Lily's printer and give them to Cian before I go. Hopefully, they'll be enough to convince him he is Croí's father.

"Ella."

"Don't, I've made up my mind. I'm leaving. When I needed him most, he gave up on me. I can't be with someone like that. If roles were reversed, I would have chosen him, no questions asked."

She lowers her head admitting defeat. "Okay, do whatever you need to do."

"Right now, I just need to sleep."

Cian

I stand on Rosie's front porch with my hands buried deep in the pockets of my grey sweatpants. My head is pounding from the whiskey myself and Ciaran consumed last night. I'm pretty sure I look worse than if I was hit by a double-decker bus.

I'm still contemplating if this is a good idea. Last night, Ciaran eventually got me to go to bed and try to sleep. He assured me giving Ella some space would be the best approach, but now that I'm standing here, I'm not so sure. I still have no idea what I'm going to say. *I'm sorry,* sure isn't going to cut it. I acted like a gobshite. Ella deserves better; I should have never questioned her like that.

I raise my hand to ring the buzzer, then pace back and forth. Fuck me, in all my life, I've never been so anxious over a closed door. Before long, the front door swings open, and I'm greeted by my favourite angry redhead. "I was wondering when you were going to show up." She has one hand resting against her hip while she sweeps the other through the air, motioning me to come in.

"Good morning to you too, Lil," I reply. I step across the threshold, just within her reach, and she slaps me in the back of the head.

"Fuck." I reach up rubbing the sting her tiny palm left.

"Before you ask, that's for overreacting. I specifically told you not to do that." Her eyes are focused on me, burning with flames that could revile a wildfire. Everyone who knows Lily knows she's a force to be reckoned with. That's why she's so good at her job. She's a tiny thing, but if you fire her up, you better be prepared for the wrath of a hurricane. She has brought bigger men than me to their knees with just a look.

"Is she here?" I ask, my gaze directed to the floor. I'm not a vulnerable person, but Ella brings that out in me. I'm still unsure if that is a good or a bad thing. I've no idea how she is going to react and that scares me shitless.

"She is, but she doesn't want to talk to you. Can't say I blame her either. What the hell was your pig head thinking?"

She folds her arms across her chest. She leans back against the narrow hall table.

I run my hand through my black hair. "Honestly, I wasn't thinking. I just reacted. The words of that article gripped a hold of my chest and wouldn't let go."

She releases a frustrated breath. Her eyes roll so far back in her head they could see the wall behind her. "Cian, you know I love you. You're like the brother I never wanted but got anyway, but you seriously fucked up." Using her hand, she points in the direction of the living room.

"That girl in there cried herself to sleep. She wants to go home, and not to the house she belongs in, but the one across the Atlantic."

My stomach somersaults at that thought. She can't leave. It would break me. My eyes weld shut, my teeth clenching as I swallow back the ball of anxiety bubbling up my throat. I suck in a calming breath through my nose, blowing it back out past my lips. "What do I do, Lily? I'm genuinely at a loss here."

"Give her time, Cian. She will come to you when she's ready." She places her hand on my forearm, offering me comfort but it doesn't help. I can feel Ella slipping from my fingertips, and fuck, I don't know how to stop her. If it's time she wants, I'll give it to her.

"Promise you'll call me if she decides she's going to leave."

"I promise. Now please go home and shower, you smell like shit," Lily teases.

"Always with the compliments, Lil."

"You're welcome." She winks, ushering me out the door.

I'm halfway down the driveway when I hear Ella shout my name. "Cian, hold up." My feet halt in their tracks. I spin to face her and my heart leaps out of my chest. My God, she is stunning. Even in leggings and a hoodie, she is the most beautiful woman I've ever seen.

I watch her tiny frame walk towards me, her arms crossed over her chest, her shoulders curled in defeat. My eyes close briefly knowing it was me who made her withdraw into herself like that. Gone is the confident woman I know and love.

"Can we talk?" she asks, her voice so low I barely hear it. I step towards her, but she moves back, not allowing me into her personal space.

"I'm sorry." The words leave my mouth before I can process what I want to say next.

"Look, Cian. I just wanted to say I'm leaving tonight. My flight is booked." She's leaving. I try to form a sentence, but I can't. All the words I want to say get stuck in my throat. *Don't leave, I love you. I love our son. Stay. Please, please stay.*

"If you'd like, you could take Croí for the day, spend some time with him before we leave... If you don't want to, you don't have to but I," she looks down to the gravel beneath her feet. "I just, I, I thought I'd offer anyway." Her arms tighten around her middle, while I stand there staring at her like a goddamn idiot. What the hell is wrong with me?

"Okay, I'll take your silence as a no then," she turns on her heel and heads back towards the house.

"Ella," I shout. Finally, my voice decides to show up.

"I'd love to. Spend time with him that is." I shift from foot to foot. If I only get a few more hours with my boy, I'm not going to waste them. Hopefully, I can use those few hours to think of a way to convince Ella to stay.

"Okay, great. Emm, could you wait here? I'll just go get him," she asks. I nod my head and give her a small forced smile. I'm anything but happy about this situation.

"Also, would you mind if I stopped by the house later to get our stuff?"

"Yeah, sure. Whatever you need, Angel." I'll give her space, for now. But she has another thing coming if she thinks I'm letting her go without one hell of a fight.

Prepare yourself, Angel. I'm going to prove to you exactly where you belong. In my arms.

Chapter Twenty-Eight

The Pieces Don't Fit Anymore by James Morrison

Cian

After I picked Croí up from Rosie's, I took him out to Bray for the day to see the Air show that was on all weekend. He was in awe of all the planes. His eyes lit up every time they performed a new stunt or trick. As a kid, my dad would bring us out here every year to see the show; it's probably one of the best memories I have with him, and that's what I wanted today to be about, making memories with Croí, ones he will never forget. Once the show is over, we get some fish and chips and sit along the shore front watching all the fishing boats dock in the harbour.

We make it through the whole day without Croí asking questions, and now — in the middle of an ice-cream parlour — he starts the interrogation. He raises the spoonful of Minion Bubble-gum to his lips while he examines me with his stormy blue eyes.

"Do you not love my mom anymore?"

Okay, how do I tackle this? "Of course, I love your mom. I'll always love her." *Fuck me, this is torture.* How am I meant to explain this to him?

"Well, if you love her so much, why is she taking me back to 'Merica?" *Cause your old man is the biggest moron in the world, and he made a colossal mistake, one he doesn't know how to fix.*

"You said I could stay here. You promised me I could live with you forever." His words hit me like a thousand tornados, the force so intense it knocks all the air from my lungs. The tears in his eyes break me. *I did this. I tore my family apart with my idiocy.*

"C'mere buddy." I open my arms wide. He climbs from his side of the teal booth and makes his way into my arms. I wrap him up in a hug, his dark hair resting beneath my chin.

"I want that too. I really do, but sometimes moms and dads need to have some space to sort out grown-up business."

I'm doing a piss poor job of explaining this to him, but I'm so far out of my depth here. *Shit, I'm a grown man on the verge of an emotional breakdown in a public place.* "Just because you're moving back to Los Angeles doesn't mean I don't love you. I'll always love you. You're my boy."

I blink back the tears welling up in my eyes. I squeeze Croí a little tighter. He raises his head his mournful eyes lock onto mine. "Will you visit me?"

"Every chance I can get, Kid."

"I love you, Dad."

"I love you, too, Buddy. I love you, too."

|***|

I kneel on the gravel driveway in front of Rosie's house with Croí clutched tightly in my arms. Sadness grips my throat, the ball of emotion too painful to swallow. I breathe in deeply, allowing his scent to fill my nose. I force myself not to break down in front of him. He needs me to stay strong, for both of us.

The sky above is grey, matching my mood. The clouds close in, rain threatening to fall. It's like the sky knows what's coming. Ella always did believe the sky reflected the earth below, and right now, I feel like my world is in chaos. I'd often find her staring up at the stars, talking to her Nana. She once told me: *The stars light the way to heaven's boulevard.*

"I'm going to miss you, Dad," he cries. His arms squeeze my neck like a lifeline. He won't let go, and I don't want him too. His tiny body shakes in my arms as he releases his tears onto my t-shirt. The smell of his baby shampoo floods my senses. I don't know when I will get to hold my son again, so I commit every detail into my memory; the softness of his hair, the little crease of sadness between his eyes. The way his little arms cling to me for dear life. I try to keep my composure, but on the inside, I feel like I'm dying.

"It's okay, everything will be okay. I'll see you soon. I promise." I don't know who I'm trying to convince, him or me.

"Bye, Dad." He releases his grip and starts to make his way to the house.

"See you later, Alligator," I shout after him.

He turns to face me with a smile that doesn't quite reach his eyes. "In a while, Crocodile."

I stay there watching him enter the house. Rosie whispers something in his ear then comes to meet me on the driveway.

"Hey. How are you holding up?" she offers.

"Not great. Is Ella here?" I ask.

"No, she's still at your place. So, big brother... what's the plan?" She raises her brow and crosses her arms over her midsection.

"I'm letting her go. She needs space, Rosie. I can't force her to stay. I fucked up. I deserve this." I run my hand through my hair and blow out a weighty sigh.

Letting Ella go is the last thing I want to do, but I've to believe it's the right thing, even if it feels like my heart and soul are leaving my body. I can't be selfish; she needs time. I've to earn her trust again, and I will, even if it takes me a lifetime to do it.

"Cian..." She narrows her eyes at me in disappointment.

"Rosie, don't. I know. I'm not giving up, not yet. I hurt her, badly. But I also know Ella; she needs time."

"I think you are an idiot," she states.

"Yeah, well, join the club."

"For the record, I think you're making a big mistake." She turns and walks away.

I walk back to the car, with a heavy heart. I take a moment to gather my emotions before turning the key in the ignition. This is it; I think to myself. *Time to say goodbye to the love of my life.*

Ella

I've been at Cian's for two hours, packing up my new life into a suitcase. I never thought for one second this would be an easy task, but the devastation weighing on my chest is making it hard to breathe. I do one more walk around, wandering in and out of every room, basking in the memories we made over the past weeks.

Each one leaves a mark on my broken heart. Lastly, I enter our, I mean Cian's bedroom. Every moment we spent together flicks through my mind. The laughter, the love, the plans for the future, all slap me in the face. It's ironic how one tiny moment in time can change the direction of a life, or in this case, three lives.

I take hold of the handle of my suitcase and flick off the light, saying goodbye one last time. I wheel my luggage up the long hallway, silently mourning the house I thought was becoming my home. I will miss it here, but I need to do this. The press, they took it too far. They started a war I cannot win. Whatever hope Cian and I had at working things out, doesn't matter; the tabloids won't ever stop. I need to get away, away from Cian, away from the fame, away from the life I thought I could have.

When I reach the bottom of the hall, I spot Cian's large frame standing beside the main door. I don't know when he got here, but he is clearly giving me the space he knows I need.

I allow my gaze to wander over his body. His head is slumped forward in defeat. His onyx hair is dishevelled — like he spent the night running his hands through it. The same hands are now shoved into the front pockets of his grey sweatpants. He sways back and forth on the balls of his feet, something I've learnt he does when he's nervous.

I come to a halt before him, and his eyes lift from where he had been burning a hole in the floor. I take in his handsome face, trying to ingrain each and every beautiful detail into my mind for safekeeping. He looks tired; the dark black circles lining his eyes are showing his lack of sleep.

The look on his face kills me; watching him now is like witnessing my heart shatter into a million tiny pieces, each shard scattering to the floor. The hurt in his deep blue eyes rip my soul to shreds.

"Ella, I'm so sorry, you have to believe me. I know what I did was wrong. I should have spoken to you before reacting. If I could go back and change it, I would. I swear. Tell me how to fix this," he begs.

"You can't; you hurt me, Cian. More than the

words of that stupid article ever could. You honestly thought I would lie about something as important as our son. I can't; I just don't know what to do with that."

He covers his eyes with his hand, dragging his fingers down his face.

We stand there for what feels like hours, mourning what could have been. No words exchanged between us, but our hearts were speaking. Together, we're just two people who love, but that love is not enough. Two people who fought but lost the war. Two people, who thought they were meant to be but were wrong. We are just two halves of what should have been the same whole.

Tears well in my eyes; they're fighting to fall, but I can't let them, I *won't* let them. I know if I allow myself to break down, even for a second, I'll never leave.

I retrieve the envelope with the DNA results from my purse, and with a shaky hand, I hold them out for Cian to take.

"What's this?" he asks, the crease in his brow highlighting his confusion.

"That is proof that Jake Saunders is not Croí's father." His eyes close at those words.

"Ella, I..."

"Don't. Okay? I can't right now. I'll call you in a few days. We can discuss Croí and visitation then if you'd like. But, right now, I need to go, or I'll miss my flight."

He nods his head, blinking back his tears. I wrap

my arms around his stiff frame and breathe him in one last time.

"I'll always love you, Cian Mulligan."

"I'm so sorry, Angel. So, fucking sorry," he sobs into my hair.

With those last words, I back away. I open the door and start walking away from the best thing that's ever happened to me.

Chapter Twenty-Nine

Stay by Hurts

Cian

I stare down at the closed envelope Ella placed in my hands. I don't need this. I understand why she felt she had to prove Croí's paternity to me. I brought this on myself; I behaved terribly the other day. I just, I got caught up in it all. I know I shouldn't have, and trust me if I could rewind, I never would have acted the way I did. And now, she's leaving. They both are.

Mere seconds ago, she walked out the door, leaving a giant hole in my heart, shaped like her.

Nothing, I said fucking nothing. I just stood there, letting the only woman I've ever loved walk out of my life. *The award for biggest idiot known to man.... goes to Cian Mulligan.*

I can't do this. I thought I could. I thought I could

let her walk away, at least for now. I never had the intention of letting her go for good.

I'd fight for her until my last breath. I knew my actions cut her deep. On top of that, the backlash from the article pushed her overboard. It was only a matter of time before she finally broke. I know I said I'd give her space and time, but I can't do it. I can't let her leave, not until she knows how much she means to me.

Earlier, when she told me she was going back home, I thought there was nothing I could say that would fix things; I knew I couldn't right the wrongs I made. I was defeated. Left to drown in the shadows of my worst mistake.

My eyes flick between the envelope and the door. *Can I fix this? Should I at least try? Fuck it!*

I pull the door open to be greeted by torrential rain. The dark clouds hanging over earlier finally decided to give way. Even the skies can't stop their tears from coming down. The large droplets pound hard against the gravel driveway. In the distance, I can barely make her out, pulling her suitcase behind her through the heavy downpour towards the bright orange Mini Cooper she borrowed from Lily.

"ELLA!" My scream stops her in her tracks. She remains still but doesn't turn to face me.

I run, I run faster than I ever have in my entire life. I don't care about the rain bucketing down and drenching my clothes or the fact that my shirt is now welded to my skin. All I see is her, all I've ever seen — is *her.*

I reach her in double-quick time. Her face is wet with a mixture of her falling tears and rain. Her expression is a painting of hurt, her eyes full of regret. Sad but beautiful. Always so beautiful.

She averts her eyes from me, avoiding my face at all costs. She wasn't expecting me to chase her. But I've been chasing her for over six years, and I'll continue to do so for the rest of my life.

"Goddammit, Ella, look at me! Please, please, look at me." The rain gets heavier, crashing against the ground beneath us. Ella's hair is dripping wet, the loose strands of her messy bun sticking to the side of her face.

"Please," I beg. "Look at me."

Her eyes meet mine. Her hazel irises lack the happy glint I'm used to, in its place a darkened cloud of misery.

"Don't do this... don't walk away. I promised you... I promised I would never let you go. I told you I would fight for you. So here I am." I stretch my arms out wide, showing her all of me. "I am fighting with every fibre of my being."

I step forward, closing the distance between us. "Don't make me live this life without you. Because I can't. I love you, Ella. I love you so fucking much that the thought of losing you, even for one second, is tearing me apart."

She stands still, and it's hard to tell between the rain and the tears flowing freely down her cheeks. Her arms hang by her side. Her chest rises and falls with every breath she takes, but she still doesn't say a word.

"I have the whole world at my fingertips, but it means nothing without you here to share it with me. The past twenty-four hours have been hell, but they made me realize that no matter what life throws at us, we can make it because we love. We love so fucking hard. Don't let them take that away from us, don't let my stupidity tear everything we built back down."

Ella bites down into her lower lip. She closes her eyes for a split second, blinking back her tears. My words are affecting her, so I keep going.

"I know this situation isn't ideal. I know everything I did cut you deep, but listen to me... We can get through this. Do you want to know how I know we can?" I say, taking another step towards her. I cup her face gently in the palms of my hands. I search her eyes, speaking my next words directly to her soul.

"Because the best love stories aren't the ones without struggle... they're the ones that live through those struggles together because they know they're strong enough to conquer them all." My tears slide down my face, their salty taste lingering on my lips.

"I know it's easier if we just let them win, walk away from this, but I don't want easy, Ella. I want someone who is strong, fierce, loyal, and protective. Someone who will fight for me when I'm being too stubborn and pig-headed. I want you, Isabella Andrews. So please, stay. I promised you once, it was us against the world. Let me prove it. Let me love you. Let yourself love me. Mò chroí agas m'anam. You have them both. My heart and my soul."

Ella steps back, freeing herself from my touch. She turns to face the opposite direction. She lifts her hand to her face wiping away the moisture from her tears and the rain. She looks up at the night sky, and I know she's having a silent conversation with her Nana.

I step towards her, resting my hand on her shoulder, urging her to turn around. "Look at me, Ella. Look at me, and tell me you don't want to try," I force out. My voice cracks with the painful thought that this is it. She's really leaving me.

She abruptly spins, her sorrowful eyes lock onto mine. Sadness and anger highlight her face. "Why Cian?" She gestures with her hands. "Nobody wants this to work. Your dad tried to sabotage us from day one, you believed the press over me, and your so-called fans have ripped every bit of my self-confidence apart." My heart breaks at her words. I never wanted to make her feel like this. Yes, I believed that article, but I was blinded by the possibility that Croí wasn't mine. I will regret my actions until the day I die.

"The world loves you." She points to my chest. "It's me they hate. The slut who wormed her way into your bed, all so she could hitch a ride on your fame train. That's how they see me, Cian. That is how they will always see me." She raises her hands to the sky. "What's the point?"

She doesn't get it. She doesn't understand.

"The point?" I close in on her, caging her between me and Lily's car. "Okay, let me give it to you. The point is I. Love. You." I punctuate each word.

I remove the envelope with the DNA results from my pocket and wave it in front of her face. "I know I deserved you handing me these. I was a fucking idiot for even questioning you, which is why I haven't looked inside this envelope, and why I'm not going too." I'm inches away from her face now, so close I can feel her breath against my two-day-old stubble. "I know I haven't acted like it, but I don't need a piece of paper to prove our boy belongs to me." I raise the brown paper concealing the results between us. With both hands, I tear it to shreds, letting each soaked piece fall to the wet ground between us.

"Cian." Her voice breaks through the silence. "You barely know me. What has it been, two months?" I know what she is doing; she is grasping at straws, looking for any excuse to justify her walking away. I'm not going to let that happen.

I widen my stance, straighten my shoulders. I place both hands on the car behind her, locking her between my arms without touching her. "I call bullshit. I know you better than you know yourself. Like when there is music playing, you move your body without even realizing you're doing it." She looks towards the ground, her resolve breaking under my intense gaze.

Using my left hand, I lift her chin, forcing her to look at me. "When you sleep, you mumble about the list of jobs you need to do the next day." She blinks. *Good, it's working.* "I know you loved your Nana ferociously, and when she passed you felt lost." She bites her bottom lip. "What about when you read one of those soppy romance novels you love? Did you know you chew your bottom lip in anticipation of what's to come?" She blows out a breath.

"Do you want me to continue, Angel? Because I could; all fucking night. I know you, Ella. I know you well enough to know you're running because you're scared. You're scared to give yourself to me completely. You are hanging off the cliff, but you're gripping on with both hands. Just jump Ella. Just jump, and I promise you, this time, I'll be there to catch you."

"What happens if I jump and fall flat on my face?" she asks through her tears. I hate that she doubts me, but considering I am the one who put us in this position, she has every right. I've learnt my lesson; I'll never let her down again.

"You won't. I jumped a long time ago, and I promise if you jump now, I will always be there to catch you. No matter what. Just give me a chance to show you. I'll never let you down again."

I see it, the defining moment that she changes her mind. The split-second decision that decides our future, our fate. She wraps her arms around my neck. Our wet clothes stick together from the rain falling from the sky.

"Do you promise to catch me?" she whispers against my lips.

"Every single time."

I capture her lips with mine, not innocently, but hot, passionate, and ferociously. I kiss her until the world fades away. Needy but soft, our tongues dance together to a song only our bodies can hear. I rest my hand below her ear, my thumb caressing her cheek as our breaths mingle. She drags her fingers down my spine, pulling me closer until there is no space left between us. We lose ourselves in one another. Eventually, we pull apart. I rest my forehead against hers and gaze lovingly into her eyes.

"Let's go get our boy," I whisper. "Let's bring him home."

Chapter Thirty

This Christmas by Picture This

Cian

Three Months Later

Christmas Eve is one of my favourite days of the year. It's the one day where all the 4Clover families come together to celebrate, no matter what. This year we are celebrating at our house. Mine and Ella's. It's our first Christmas together as a family. Croí is so excited, I have never seen a kid that wants to go to bed early. All-day, he has been watching the clock, praying for bedtime to come.

Things have been going great for Ella and me. After that night on the driveway, we had Lily hold a press conference so we could tell our story. The real version. A love story about a boy who fell in love with a girl at first sight.

That, unfortunately, someone kept them apart, but with a bit of luck and a whole lot of love, they managed to find their way back together.

We told them about the child they share, and that the boy is the happiest he's ever been with them both by his side where they belong.

I can't wait to see the look on Croí's little face tomorrow morning. Let's just say, we may have gotten a little carried away with his Christmas presents, but that's what happens when you let four Rockstar's loose in a toy store. There was little to no budget. We each filled a shopping trolley — just for him. Everything from Nerf Guns to Drum kits — that was Ciaran's bright idea, but it won't be as funny to him when I set it up in his house and pay Croí to bang on it to his heart's content. *Fucker!*

Ella nearly passed out when she saw all the stuff we bought; but seeing him tear open everything tomorrow will be worth the ear-bashing I got for spoiling him rotten; her words not mine. It's my first Christmas as someone's dad, and I wanted to make it special. I know I may have lost the run of myself, and maybe I was a bit excessive with his gifts, but I have six years of missed Christmases to make up for. No expense was spared. You can't put a price on making memories.

Rosie and Mam organized for the house to be decorated, head-to-toe Christmas. Just think Pinterest on steroids. I wanted everyone to feel like they were fucking sitting in Lapland. They didn't disappoint; the place looks amazing. When I brought Ella back to see it, there were genuine tears in her beautiful hazel eyes. She never had a big

Christmas because, for years, she had to live paycheck to paycheck.

I want to make this year a memorable one, a day she will never forget. The garden is lit up with large candy canes that line the driveway, and white outdoor fairy lights are strung through the trees, starting at the entrance of the property and ending at the pathway into the house. Icicle lights flash across the rooftop, making the house visible from the sky. It looks like something from a movie. The inside of the house is a replica of Santa's lair. Mammy Mulligan bought every decoration she could find — Croí is her first grandchild, so she went all out.

There are Santa's, elves, snowmen, nutcrackers, trains — you name it and she bought it. Even the big man in the red suit would be jealous of this festive pad. We even have Christmas cushion covers and rugs, for fuck's sake. The large stone mantle is adorned with Christmas stockings. One for every member of our large band family. A ten-foot Christmas tree — real of course — sits in the big bay window, giving off the perfect balsam tree scent.

Lights — matching the ones outside — light up the tree branches, making all the New Bridge Silver ornaments glisten. The fire is crackling, filling the room with the soft glow of embers. Mistletoe is hung in every doorway, giving me an excuse to kiss Ella every two seconds. The place looks magical, and Croí absolutely loves it. I stand in the doorway, looking around the room and taking in all the faces.

Ciaran and Lily are sitting on the floor on either side of the coffee table. They're fighting over a game of Cluedo. Nothing new there. Rosie and Cillian are seated beside the fire, heads close together in deep conversation. Conor and Cassie are on the L shaped couch, laughing at the movie playing on the TV — Home Alone. A Christmas classic. The love of my life is tucked safely under my arm. It's quickly become her favourite place to be, mine too.

Finally, Mam and Croí are curled up on the armchair reading 'The night before Christmas.' Joy — it's the only way to describe how I'm feeling right now. The only person missing is my Dad, and honestly, nobody misses that asshole. I cut him out of my life completely after everything he did to this family. We deserved better than his lies. He was only out for his own gain, and ironically, it left him on his own in the end.

I spot Cillian making his way to the kitchen, and he catches my eye, letting me know it's time. I place a small gentle kiss on Ella's forehead. "Why don't you go keep Rosie company? I've got to help Cillian with something." Her arms wrap around my waist squeezing me tight. She stands on her tippy-toes and kisses my cheek. "Sure thing, handsome. Don't be long, though; it's nearly time for Croí to go to bed." "I won't, I'll be right back. I want to tuck him in."

|***|

Fuck me, I'm sweating! I've been waiting for this moment for weeks. I never anticipated it would be this nerve-wracking.

I quickly make my way to where Cillian is waiting — not so patiently — in the kitchen. "Do you have it?" I panic. "Would you relax? Of course, I have it." He laughs, taking pleasure from my current state. Just wait until it's his turn. I will torture that fucker to no end.

He hands me the small red velvet box, the one I have been hiding from Ella for the last two months. It feels heavy in my hands, maybe because it holds the weight of my future.

"What if she says no?" I ask, uncertainty creeping in.

"She won't. Anyone with two eyes can see the love you both have for each other. You have this, man." He squeezes my shoulder in a reassuring gesture. I release a breath.

Jesus Christ, I've planned this for weeks, every detail, every word I would say; all I can hope for now is for her to say yes.

"Do you have your guitar ready? I want you to play 'Moment' first." Moment is the song we recorded a few months back. The one I wrote for Ella. She hasn't heard it yet. I've been saving it for this very reason.

"Yeah, all set. Ready whenever you are," Cillian states. I nod my head and make my way back to the sitting room with Cillian not far behind me.

I'm ready, ready to ask the most important

question of my life. I clear my throat, grabbing the attention of everyone in the room. Eight sets of eyes narrow in on me, and I feel the pressure of what I am about to do hit me like a ton of bricks.

"Sorry for the interruption, but I have something I want to share." I pull my hand out gesturing for Ella to join me. She stands, hesitant for a moment before meeting me in the middle of the room. I signal Conor, and he quickly places a chair behind where Ella currently stands.

"Sit, please," I ask.

"What's going on?" she whispers. Her eyes dart around the room. I place a kiss on her forehead.

"Patience, Angel." I give her my signature smile, and she seems to relax a bit. Slowly, she sits back into the chair. Her eyes dart from me to Rosie, questioning what's going on. Rosie shrugs her shoulders. *I've no idea.*

"Okay, so I know you're all wondering what the hell I'm up to, so I'll cut right to it. Recently, I wrote a song. Everyone here knows that's usually Cillian's domain, but this song, I wrote for Ella. I thought now would be the perfect time to share it with you all.

"You ready, Buddy?" I ask Croí. He nods his head. Excitement is written all over his face. He climbs down from my mother's lap and rushes over to Cillian, who hands him another small acoustic guitar. They've been practicing the melody together in secret. He was over the moon when I asked him if I could marry his mom. He asked me if he could help, and I couldn't deny him.

Cillian and Croí both begin to strum the soft melody of 'Moment' together. Ella has a beaming smile on her face as she watches Croí with his eyebrows furrowed in concentration; it's adorable. She loves to see Croí playing the guitar, and I have to say he is pretty good for a six-year-old. I move around to stand in front of Ella. I take her hand in mine and look straight into her eyes. I begin singing the lyrics to her, pouring my heart into each and every word.

Saw you from across the bar,
I didn't know your name.
I knew that you were special,
there was something 'bout your face.
I started walking towards you,
to introduce myself.
You crashed right into me,
one moment, and I fell.

Tears fill her hazel eyes as she stares up at me in wonder. I can tell that she is reminiscing about the night we met. I can't believe it's been nearly seven years since I first laid eyes on my forever.

When the night was over,
I didn't wanna go.
I took your hand in mine and asked you, "Could I walk you home?"
We walked and talked for hours,
I told you all my dreams.
It was at that moment I knew you were meant for me.

Her tears are sliding down her cheeks, but the

smile on her face lets me know that they are happy ones. Everyone else in the room has vanished, all I see is her. "I love you," she mouths. I kiss her hand before continuing.

Years have separated us,
my feelings never changed,
Lady Luck, she brought you back into my arms again.
This time, it is forever,
and I want you to know,
now you're back in my life, I'm never letting go.
So, Angel, can you give me,
this one moment that I seek.
I'll promise you forever, my soul and heart to keep.

I get down on one knee before her and her eyes widen. I pull the ring box from my pocket, and a gasp leaves her lips. I open the lid, revealing the four-carat diamond ring my Mam and sister helped pick out. Ella's eyes widen even further, and her hands move to cover her mouth.

I'm asking you this question.
The biggest of my life.
I'm on one knee as I ask thee,
will you be my wife?

Ella

I'm shaking; I can't believe this.

That ring, oh my God.

This was the last thing I was expecting. I'm going to be Mrs. Ella Mulligan. I open my mouth to answer his question, but before I can, Cian silences me with a finger. *What the hell is he doing?*

"Don't answer... not yet. First, I have a few things I need to say." I nod my head. This is so surreal. Cian gazes up at me from his spot on the floor.

"Ella, I love you. I never believed in love at first sight, but then you crashed into me at a stupid love lock night, and immediately, I was a goner. I fell — ass over face — in love with a beautiful girl in a red dress. I can't explain it, but I just knew, right then, you were the one for me." He releases a breath and reaches up to wipe the tears cascading down my face.

"It was as if my soul recognized you before I did. The next morning when I woke to find you gone, I felt this certain emptiness I can't quite describe. I was incomplete, like there was a piece missing. For years, I tried to fill that space, but nothing or no one ever could fill the hole inside me. It belonged to you."

My heart is pounding in my chest, each beat ricocheting through my ears. "It wasn't until I found you again that I felt like I could finally breathe. The moment I saw you standing before me, I knew I wasn't ever going to let you walk out of my life. Not again. We missed years together due to reasons beyond our control, but I promise, if you'll let me, I will make up for every minute that we spent apart. If you say yes, I promise I will fight for you, for us."

I squeeze his hand, letting him know I will too. "I'll compromise and sacrifice if need be. I love you enough to believe in us, who we are together and who we are as individuals. I know that together, we are strong enough to survive any storm life gives us. My love for you has only deepened with every passing day, and I know that when I'm old and grey, struggling for my last breath, I will look back at my life and I'll cherish every single moment because I got to share them all with you."

My god, I'm a mess. "So, Isabella May Andrews, would you please do me the honour and become my wife?" Yes, Yes, Yes! I nod my head, too consumed by my emotions to form words. Cian's speech hits me right in the heart. He is an amazing man, an amazing father. He's the love of my life. I look into his deep blue eyes, and I know I want to spend the rest of my life loving this man.

I lost myself when we lost each other all those years ago, and since he found me again, he has loved me back to life.

I grab his face between my hands. I rest my forehead against his. Still holding his gaze, I whisper my answer against his lips. "Yes, all the freaking yes's"

His strong arms wrap around me, pulling me from my seat. My arms find their way around his neck, holding me up. My legs wrap around his waist as he spins me around the room. Cheers erupt around us from all our family and friends. I have never been so happy in all my life. I look up at the ceiling, sharing this moment with the one person I know is watching from above. *Nana, I found him. My calm. My soulmate. My soon-to-be husband. I just wish you had the chance to meet him too.*

"Mom, Dad, look! It's snowing," Croí shouts running towards the window. I take it as a sign, one that says Nana heard me.

I hear her voice as it rings loud in my head. *"Find your calm, Ella, and when you do, don't ever let him go."*

The End

Acknowledgements

To Joshua & Benjamin, although I hope you never read this, this one is for you. As your mother, I try to encourage you to follow your dreams. But, how can I expect that of you when I was too afraid to follow my own. So, this is me, shooting for the sky, feeling the fear and doing it anyway. One day, when you are both older, I hope you will do the same.

To my wild at heart mother, thank you for showing me that without struggle, we can never truly be strong. For teaching me to never let anyone dim my sparkle; and that the "f word" is not a curse but a sentence enhancer. Love your favourite child.

To my family and friends, I love you all. There is way too many to name, but you know who you are. Thanks for supporting me on this crazy ride. Sorry if I became a hermit, ignoring all your calls. I promise to answer now. (Kidding, the next book won't write itself)

To Lilly M Henderson and Ava Morgan my wonderful editors. I cannot thank you both enough for all the time and effort you put into making this book readable. Thank you, for your patience, your time and most of all your support throughout this 4Clover journey. I appreciate every comma, every em-dash and every "show don't tell" you threw at me.

To Danielle Paul, thank you for holding my hand, and for being my rock when I was on the verge of giving up. You truly are an earth angel. I cannot wait for the day I get to meet you, for real, and not over the internet.

To Elle Maxwell, without you, my social media game would be weak. Thank you for teaching me all things tech. You helped me get this book across the finish line, you designed everything, from promo images to this amazing cover, and for that, I will forever be grateful. Check out her book Us, again. It's available on Amazon NOW! You will not be disappointed.

To Daria, my soul sister. I'm so glad I found you on the little, strange, orange website that is Wattpad. All the love for you and all your crazy. Thank you for being my biggest supporter. You've done so much to promote my work and I love you so much for it. You truly are the greatest friend.

To all the other Wattpad ladies, I love you all. Thanks for pushing me (in a good way) to publish. This book is dedicated to all of you.

To my Wattpad family (The best of Wattpad Ladies), without you, this book would've never reached its full potential. Thank you for giving me the push I needed, and for pulling me out of meltdown mode on more than one occasion; Most importantly, sending me all those hot Insta pages when I was lacking inspiration. I love you all.

A big thank you to all the bloggers and readers who took the time to read this book. I appreciate it so much. Please leave a review on any (or if you're feeling generous) all, of my social media platforms.

Much Love Shauna xXx

Connect with
Shauna Mc Donnell

Enjoyed Luck? Make sure you stay in the loop!

Join my reading group: Shauna's Steam Queenz.

Follow me on Instagram.

Like my author page.

Find me on Goodreads.

Excerpt from Love, 4Clover Book Two

Prologue
Mr. Almost by Meghan Trainor

<u>Starz Unveiled</u>

Sean and Rosie are getting hitched!
Well, ladies and gentlemen, today is the day.
The biggest wedding of the year is finally here.
The only daughter of Michael Mulligan, (4Clovers
manager and part owner of Sham Rock Records) and the
son of Patrick Morgan, (founder of Ireland's largest
entertainment law firm, Morgan & Son) tie the knot.
The extravagant ceremony is set to take place in the
spectacular gardens of the Powerscourt Hotel Resort Spa,
at two p.m.
The guest list for this special day is jam-packed with
A-listers, including Ireland's hottest indie rock band,
4Clover. The band's lead singer, Cian Mulligan (the
bride-to-be's brother) will be amongst many of the famous
faces in attendance today. A source close to the band has

said although lead guitarist, and close childhood friend of the family, Cillian O'Shea, has flown back to Dublin for the big day, he will not be attending the wedding ceremony. We at Starz Unveiled are wondering why that is?

We have been led to believe, that Mr. O'Shea and Mr. Morgan do not see eye to eye. We can't help but wonder if the history between the raven-haired beauty and the broody musician is the cause?

What do you think, readers?

Rosie

*W*ell, today is the day.

The day most little girls dream of.

The dream dress, the dream venue, and most importantly, the dream man.

You guessed it; it is my wedding day. But, contrary to what my younger, more naive, ten-year-old self thought—this is not the dream day I once envisioned it to be.

I am not radiating happiness, and that I'm so in love glow everyone blabs on about, is virtually non-existent.

There are no nervous jitters, no sweaty palms, no butterflies of anticipation fluttering around my stomach.

Just complete emptiness.

Let's just say, my feet are so far beyond cold, I can no longer feel them.

I'm so numb, I can't even appreciate the fine details, the intricate design, the beautiful decor. I'm an interior designer for Christ's sake, detail is my Nutella. I live for that shit. But, no… this nightmare wedding has sucked the joy right out of my happiness, making what was meant to be the happiest day of this girl's life, possibly the worst.

I should be impatiently waiting to walk down the aisle into the arms of my happily ever after. Instead, I am camped out, sulking in an outrageously large marble bathtub, in an overpriced, vintage lace, Vera Wang gown. Hiding from the reality of what in the actual fuck did I sign myself up for.

Today, I should marry the man of my dreams, my best friend, the person I want to build the rest of my life with, not the man of my father's dreams.

Alas, here we are, mere hours away from my inevitable nuptials and I'm spiralling. When exactly my love life turned into a business transaction, I'm not quite sure.

All I know is, it's unavoidable. A necessary evil to help protect someone I once — and if I'm being completely honest — still love. When I envisioned this day throughout my teenage years — we all do, don't deny it — was it my soon-to-be husband's face I saw waiting for me at the altar? No, it was not.

Who did I see?

The man of my actual dreams, the same man who haunts my subconscious whether I want him to, or not.

Cillian O'Shea, 4Clovers lead guitarist, my best friend's older brother; and my brother Cian's best friend. Cillian was my first kiss, my first love, my first heartbreak. He was my first everything. I know what you're all thinking. It's a little too late for me to be questioning my life choices, and you're right. But, let's get one thing straight… this was not my choice.

I was given an ultimatum; one I could not refuse. Also, I know most arranged marriages went out of fashion in the eighteen-hundreds or whatever, but when Michael Mulligan wants something, he stops at nothing to get it. Even if that means his daughter will be miserable for the rest of her life.

Here's the thing about Sean, he is boring. Personally, I've had more exciting conversations with myself. The only thing he really has going for him, is his looks.

Without sounding extremely vain right now, the man is a solid eight. But, is he marriage material?

Most definitely not.

So, my guess is, you're all wondering how I ended up with the knight dressed in shiny aluminium foil, instead of my one and only true Prince Charming?

Well, let's take it back to the beginning and find out.

Available Now on Amazon!

Cillian & Rosie's Story.

Printed in Poland
by Amazon Fulfillment
Poland Sp. z o.o., Wrocław